Jessie Fothergill

From Moor Isles

a love story - Vol. 2

Jessie Fothergill

From Moor Isles
a love story - Vol. 2

ISBN/EAN: 9783337409685

Printed in Europe, USA, Canada, Australia, Japan

Cover: Foto ©Andreas Hilbeck / pixelio.de

More available books at **www.hansebooks.com**

FROM MOOR ISLES.

A LOVE STORY.

BY

JESSIE FOTHERGILL,

AUTHOR OF

"THE FIRST VIOLIN," "KITH AND KIN," ETC.

IN THREE VOLUMES.
VOL. II.

LONDON:

RICHARD BENTLEY AND SON,

Publishers in Ordinary to Her Majesty the Queen.

1888.

CONTENTS OF VOL. II.

PART III.

PART IV.

PART III.

FROM MOOR ISLES.

CHAPTER I.

HOW LUCY WENT TO CHURCH.

WHILE Ines Grey was all unconsciously going through her love-story, drinking of its mingled sweetness and bitterness, without distinctly realizing what the mixture was, which was yet so intoxicating and so irresistible, there was another love-story —quite as vivid, quite as intensely lived through by the actors in it, going on in and around Moor Isles. The one day there whose history has been given was merely a parenthesis in the sentence, as it were—after it was over, Brian was quickly engrossed again and more deeply than before in the persons and in the passion which had for some time been over-mastering him. That day which had been so bright and so apart (if he had ever read " Poems in Prose," he might, in think-ing of that day, have recalled that perfectly beautiful and perfectly sad one, " How lovely and fresh those roses were!" but he was unacquainted with that little gem of fancy and genius)—that day was over, gone ; had passed away into the limbo of things which have been and are now no more. Brian might also have laid to heart the song which Felix had sung as his last contribution that night, in which came the words—

" Sie singet, Herr des Hauses, verschliess das Thor,
   Dass nicht die Welt, die Alte, dring ins Gemach."

On the contrary, Brian threw wide open

the door, and "die Welt, die Alte" was soon, very soon with him again, as it had been before.

Lucy Barraclough had gone down to Moor Isles that evening, unaware (despite Alice Ormerod's suspicion) that Brian was not alone, but dimly conscious there was some hostile influence at work against her, and with her vanity hurt by Brian's absence from her side, of nearly three days' duration. She had resolved to bring him back to his allegiance, or, in her own phraseology, "to know the reason why." Before finding that he had visitors, she had mentally accused Alice Ormerod of being the cause of his defection, and that must not be allowed for a moment. She soon found out the real state of things, but that made no difference. He had been recalcitrant—he must be brought once more into a state of due submission and humility.

The first step towards this consummation, of course, was to drag him away instantly from his own abode and bring him to Jessamine Lawn to spend the evening there. How they went thither in company has been related. When they had been assembled some little time Jim proposed a game at billiards—for why should not the proceeds of a railway grease manufactory be metamorphosed into the cheerful semblance of a green-cloth covered table of the best make, and charming ivory balls clicking pleasantly and sharply as they flew about hither and thither, under the blows of the cues? Brian was no very brilliant performer on this particular instrument—his hands, and his head too, were better adapted for evoking moving strains from his violin, but he loved to think he could cope with the best of them, and if he ever lost—why, of course, one had to lose

sometimes.   But to-night he won.   He
was excited; he talked and laughed a good
deal—he made some wonderful flukes, but
—he won.   They played for money, but
not for very high stakes.   When the playing ceased, Brian was the gainer of some
three pounds, ten shillings, part of which
he had won from Jim Barraclough, and
the other part from a friend of Jim's, who
had appeared on the scene soon after they
had begun to play—one Richard, or, as he
was generally called, " Dicky," Law; an
oldish young man, with a very delicate,
smooth complexion, which would have put
to shame that of many a dainty girl; sandy,
almost red hair—not much of it—and
whiskers, handsome regular features, and
blue eyes—very curious eyes were those
of this dubious Dicky Law—they were
rather near together, and had the most
remarkable trick of always seeming to slide

into position when they met those of other
people. And sometimes, when he had
been silent for a considerable time—for he
was not loquacious—if one happened to
look at him, one would find his eyes just
sliding away from one's face. He had a
flannel business near Hollowley, and was
sprung from exactly the same class as the
Barracloughs themselves; but by hook or
by crook, he had contrived to be very
much better educated than they were—to
be, in fact, so far as mere modern knowledge goes, well-educated. He had none
of their broad, vulgar tricks of accent and
expression; he had a great many books,
went in for the improvement of the masses,
the elevation of women, the extension of
the franchise; was likewise what by a Scot
would be called "theologically free," and
had many other advanced notions on
civilization and social questions; and yet

there were people—Brian was one of them
—to whom the brutal ignorance of the
Barracloughs—their horizon bounded by
the amount of money they could turn over
in a year, and their sublime indifference
to every amenity of life of the finer and
more refined kind—were less displeasing
than the more polished personality of
Dicky Law. Brian was well aware of the
failings of the Barraclough mankind ; he
went there to see Lucy, not them, and he
often wondered why Law, who professed
to despise ignorance and vulgarity, was
such a constant visitor at the house. He
had more than once expressed his wonder
at the fact, and his dislike of the man, to
Lucy, who shrugged her shoulders and
said—

"Oh, he's awfully stupid, is Dicky!
But Jim says he plays a good hand at
whist, and his billiards aren't so bad either.

And Jim must have his whist and his billiards, or his pool, you know. You needn't notice him."

Yet Brian had allowed himself to be drawn into playing with him this evening, and, as has been said, retired from the contest the winner of a small sum. Spirits and water and cigars were going freely while the game went on, and Lucy was present the whole time, even playing one short game with Brian, while the other two professed to look up some business details relative to the state of the Irkford market the day before. Brian lost that time. Lucy played a very neat little game, but, as she sweetly said, it was for love, not money, so it did not matter. It was late—after one in the morning—when the party broke up, with a promise on Brian's part either to come again on Monday, or else to meet them at the "Swan,"

in Hollowley, for pool.   He went away to
his own house, leaving Law behind, he
having arrived to spend what was there
called "the week-end"—Saturday and
Sunday nights—at Jessamine Lawn.

When Brian had gone, Lucy, giving
way to the feelings of weariness and
sleepiness which had for some time almost
overcome her, yawned long and rather
loudly, stretched out her arms, and remarked —

"Well, if you two fellows mean to keep
it up any longer, I don't.   I'm tired, and
I'm going."

"Stop a bit, Lucy," said Jim, with a
meaning look ; "wait till I come back."

"No, I shan't," she answered, with a
sudden, swift decisiveness, as the sleepiness
vanished and a look of displeasure came
over her face ; and, before he could leave
the room, she was at the door, waving her

hand slightly to them, and saying "Good-night," she vanished.

"You're not half sharp enough," said Dicky Law to his friend; and it was astonishing to see what a black look spread itself over his delicate pink and white complexion, and came into his light blue eyes.

"Perhaps I didn't want to be," retorted Jim, indifferently. "I don't know what you may be made of, but I've had a long day, and so has Lucy, for that matter. For God's sake, drop the game for a few hours, and let's get a bit of sleep. There's all to-morrow before you."

He spoke sulkily. A slight, gentle smile crossed the face of the other man, but he said nothing. Jim busied himself in extinguishing the oil-lamps with which the table had to be lighted, for it goes without saying that gas was unknown at

Thornton-in-Ravenside.   After doing this,
he took up a smaller lamp which stood on
a table near the door, and led the way
into the hall.   Every one had gone to bed
but themselves.   Jim turned out more
lights, leaving, however, one or two on the
different landings and staircases, and they
finally parted, going into their respective
rooms.   After which, the stillness of the
remote country—an absolute, unbroken,
palpitating stillness—settled over Jessamine
Lawn, as over every other house in the
neighbourhood, and the small hours of the
Sunday morning gradually grew larger as
the inmates of the house slept, or waked,
as the case might be.

*   *   *   *   *

The Barraclough men were not at church
on Sunday morning ; but Lucy was.   She
seldom missed attending divine worship
once, at any rate, each week.   Fresh as a

rose, with her pale face and dark eyes, and her exquisitely neat attire and most becoming bonnet, she left the house be- times, and lightly tripped the half-mile that lay between Jessamine Lawn and the parish church of Thornton-in-Ravenside. No venerable, hoary fane, this, but an entirely Philistine and entirely hideous structure, erected in some year of the thirties. Its style could hardly be called debased, because it had none to be debased. It was, if one may say so, a specimen of insignificance so extreme as to be intense. Its interior rose from insignificance into the more positive quality of hideousness. Naked white walls, with here and there a ghastly black marble slab adorned with the usual white relief urn, and weeping willow, and floppy looking female figure engaged in industriously filling the urn with solid marble tears ; long, plain win-

dows filled with diamond panes of a spotty,
greenish-white glass ; immense, high-walled
pews, the object of whose structure appeared to be to conceal their temporary
inmates as much as possible from one
another, as though they had met for some
object of which they were thoroughly
ashamed, and were desirous of, unseen,
accomplishing their fell purposes.   And
yet it would seem that they had an uneasy
consciousness all the time of being observed ; or perhaps it was the existence of
that observation which had caused them
to build their pew-walls so high—but, at
any rate, on the wall on each side of
the altar, there was a large black board,
with a portion of the Ten Commandments
inscribed upon it in golden letters, and at
the top of each board was depicted the
similitude of a huge glaring eye, also in
gold, with fierce golden rays streaming

away from and around it—the most utterly frightful, senseless, and hideous illustration perhaps ever offered by the most hopelessly perverse misunderstander of symbolical art that ever existed—the ecclesiastical architect as he flourished during the early years of the reign of her present Majesty.

Lucy sat in the great square pew "belonging" to Jessamine Lawn, and exactly confronted one of the gilded eyes. She had gone to Thornton church now for some three or four years—the Barracloughs were not natives of Thornton, only settlers therein—and she knew that the eye was there—indeed, she had often gazed at it, and when the sermon was long and uninteresting, she had amused herself by following its gigantic curves, and trying to count the rays that emanated from it. She had often succeeded in soothing herself almost or quite to sleep by this process, but it had never occurred to her how hideous the thing was—or how ludicrous. That was not the kind of thing that interested or amused Lucy Barraclough.

So here she sat on this particular Sunday morning, as she had often sat before, with her little Russia leather case of books, ready to follow the parson in all his proceedings, and quite ready, too, to watch the different members of the congregation as they dropped in. It was not a numerous • congregation; Lucy knew them all by sight and by name, if not personally, and as, one after another, they appeared, her eyes rested on each of them, and the expression of her face was unchanged, though in her mind there was excitement, and the constant wonder, "Will she come? Will he come? I hope they will—but he won't—no."

At last her eye fell upon two persons
just entering; the upright, stately figure
of Alice Ormerod, and the somewhat
stooping, but still huge and stalwart stature
of her father.

"Ah! there *she* is!" Lucy said to herself, giving a little involuntary pat of
satisfaction to the bow of her bonnet-
strings. She did not think Brian would
be there, and, indeed, he put in no appearance. Alice and her father sat where she,
almost unseen, could observe them; and
she did so, and saw how Alice's proud face
was sad, and paler, too, than usual. The
sight gladdened her. It was soothing to
her feelings, inasmuch as it showed that
her interference the evening before had
produced a distinct effect, just where she
had wished that such effect should be
produced. She knew perfectly well that
Brian's heart was her own; that Alice had,

as she put it, "no chance in the world"
with him. She knew that, by lifting her
little finger, she could beckon him in the
flash of an eye from Alice's side to her
own. All this she knew perfectly well.
But she knew also that Alice loved him,
while she, Lucy, did not; and though she
had no faintest capacity in herself for a
high, unselfish love, yet she dimly felt that
such a love was in its way a powerful kind
of thing, and she was jealous of it—jealous •
that another should possess a weapon
which she would never know how to handle.
Conscious that Alice was mistress of this
great instrument of unselfishness, Lucy
was angry and suspicious of every word
spoken by Brian to Alice, of every civil
look he might give to the young woman;
and the discovery, the night before, of
their helpful, sociable intercourse, had filled
her with a deep, uneasy anger and vexa-

tion.   She had at once resorted to her
own weapons—those which she could
wield with ease and address—had dragged
Brian away from under the very eyes of
the other woman, whose love made her
shy and miserable in the presence of one
who knew it and despised it.   Lucy had
not seen how Alice, with sunken head
and drooping shoulders, had slipped away
from Moor Isles to the privacy of her own
home, but she had guessed at her departure.   That, however, was not enough.
Alice must be punished, and Brian must
be punished, for presuming to be together
without her knowledge, and for having
common acquaintance unknown to her.

"If that's the consequence of his going
to these precious concerts," Lucy decided
within herself, as she knelt on her knees,
and half-sang, half-said, the Lord's Prayer,
after the parson—"if that's the consequence,

he will just have to give them up.   I'll see
whether I can't make him.   We will try
which wins—the concert, or an evening in
my company.   I remember Alice saying
how very good it was for him to go—how
it took him amongst different kinds of
things and people.   I dare say.   We will
see whether some of his friends up at
Thornton are not enough for him.   Those
two women yesterday"—Lucy's face flushed
—"she had been making up to them, I •
could see.   As if they were *her* sort.   I'm
certain she prevented him from asking me
to meet them.   Very well—'For Thine is
the kingdom, the power, and the glory, for
ever and ever.   Amen.'"

When the service was over, she walked
out of her pew and down the aisle, looking
almost quakerlike in her soft, dove-coloured
gown of silk and cashmere, though the
crimson carnations in her bonnet were of a

more worldly taste. Lucy understood very
well the colours and the shapes of things
which best suited her, though she might be
somewhat left to herself occasionally in the
matter of some particular style of garment
for a given occasion. But this morning
the colour, cut, and material of her costume were all irreproachable, and, as she
cast a side-glance upon the three stiff-
looking daughters of the Squire of the
neighbourhood—the Misses Dunstan, each
of whom wore the colour least suited to her
particular style and complexion, she felt at
once a contempt for them and a content
with her own more satisfactory arrangements which, if she had been a cat, would
doubtless have expressed itself in a loud
purring, but which in a woman, and one
who was in church, had to be satisfied
with looks only.

Hapless Misses Dunstan! Yet there

were persons who found them delightful ;
and all Lucy's pleasure in the superior
elegance of her own attire, all her consciousness of how much richer her father
was than Mr. Dunstan, did not quite
sweeten the fact that, while these ill-
dressed young women took no notice
whatever of her—Lucy—she noticed all
three, and their father as well, give the
most friendly of nods and smiles to Alice
and Farmer Ormerod. They would ex•
change some talk outside the church, she
knew. And she was not going to stand
by and see it, so she walked a little more
quickly, but with no appearance of un-
seemly haste, to the door ; she stepped
outside, and was about to proceed serenely
on her way, when she encountered a pair
of gliding blue eyes, and the voice of Dicky
Law said—

" So I'm just in time, it seems, to have

the pleasure of walking home with you. Quite in luck's way, I declare!"

The smile faded from Lucy's face. A very grave expression succeeded it; it was not in a very spirited voice that she made her retort.

"So you've actually managed to be up and dressed, and at the church door by twelve o'clock! I should think no one ever heard of such a thing happening to you before."

" To have the pleasure of walking home with you, as I said," he repeated, smiling; and, without asking further leave, walked on by her side.

They left the churchyard, and turned into the road in the direction of home. When about half-way there, they passed Brian's house, with the farm just beyond it. All was still and quiet, with the stillness of a country Sunday morning. Through the lattice-work blind which was before the lower part of the kitchen window, was dimly discernible the respectable figure of Sarah Stott, moving to and fro, bent on household concerns. Other sign of life there was none. Lucy raised her eyes, slackened her pace, and looked openly and with interest at the little old mansion.

"It's the nicest old house there is any-where about here," she observed reflec-tively, yet decidedly. "It's the sort of house I could do to live in. Somehow I don't care for new houses, like ours."

"Then why don't you make haste to settle yourself there?" asked Dicky, his lips growing a little tight.

Lucy shook her head, with a little laugh.

"If I could settle there alone—but not with Brian Holgate," said she, with the appearance, at any rate, of the most artless candour, "with his fiddling and his singing, and his temper never two days alike—and nothing to do," she added, with rare practical wisdom, "except squander the bit of money that his father left him—no."

"Then, if you don't mean to have him, why don't you let him alone?" asked Dicky again.

"I don't know that I meddle with him. It's he that doesn't let me alone," said Lucy.

"You know very well what I mean."

"Well, perhaps I do. You mean, why don't I make him go about his business? No; that would just mean turning him over to Alice Ormerod"—she looked with no friendly expression into the farmyard which they were passing—"and that," she added, with quiet vindictiveness, "I never will. With her piety and her pride, setting herself up to be better than other people.

That Alice Ormerod is beyond everything with her airs—telling Brian that he was going to ruin by coming so much to us. She meant to me, I know. And he believed her too, and does believe her."

" Perhaps because it's true," said Dicky, encouragingly. "But do you mean he told you what she had said? *What* a fool he must be!"

"I never said who had told me. I know she said it; and true or not, I'll never forgive her!" said Lucy.

"And how long do you mean to carry on this kind of game—playing fast and loose with him and with me?" asked her companion searchingly. "How do you know that Miss Ormerod—she's a handsome girl, by the way—would make three of such as you—how do you know she would look at your precious Brian?"

There was an unpleasant sneer in his

voice.   Lucy's laugh was no pleasanter as
she answered——

"Pooh! I know her sort. She's in
love with him. That means, that everything he does that's wrong and silly is
not his fault, but some one else's—mine,
because he happens to be in love with me.
If he happened to be in love with some
one else, it would be that some one else's
fault."

"You seem to have gone into the subject pretty deeply."

"I have. I've been obliged to. She
shall not have him unless——"

"Unless what?"

Dicky spoke calmly, and Lucy was not
looking at him at the moment, or she
might have seen how ferociously his eyes
glided to and fro in his excitement. She
was pursuing her own train of thought——
that which had been in her mind during

the whole of the morning service at church, and she spoke her thoughts now, without much reference to Dicky, except that she knew talking to him about Brian staved off the necessity of having to listen while he talked about herself to her.

" Unless he got to be worthless, as you might say—not worth looking at or speaking to ; then she might take him, for aught I cared.'

" You mean, if he'd lost house and land, such as he has, and his money, and couldn't hold up his head, and was low down, like—like this," said Dicky, kicking a tuft of grass by the roadside, and unconsciously quoting almost the exact words of another—a greater, but not a more unscrupulous than himself, the artless and accomplished Veitel Itzig.

" Yes, that's what I mean," said Lucy, tranquilly. " If he was too sick and sorry

to care who took him up, and if I knew
that he'd given me the best he had to give,
why then she might have him, when he
was worth nothing to any one else. But
there," she added quickly, " what nonsense
to talk of such things ! They don't happen
nowadays. Brian has his house and his
property; he's comfortable enough in a
small way—except when I make him uncomfortable. But I wish him no harm ;
it's Alice Ormerod I can't do with.
Nothing would hurt her so much as for
him to be hurt."

"Oh, you women !" ejaculated the
virtuous Dicky. "To wish to see a girl ,
like that Alice Ormerod brought low, who
has never done you an evil turn, except
by caring a little too much for a gaping
young idiot, who you think ought to be
dangling at your apron-strings. It's
horrible—perfectly horrible !"

He shook his head over the enormity
of it. "Now tell me, Lucy," he added, as
they paced about in the garden of Jessamine Lawn, for they had now arrived
there—"tell me one thing—when will
you marry *me*?"

"Oh, there's time enough to talk about
that!" said Lucy, uneasily. She always
was more or less uneasy in this man's
presence—at any rate, when she was alone
with him.

"When your fine young Holgate, or
your dear Miss Ormerod, is biting the
dust?" he asked, in quiet, gentle tones.

She was silent.

"Eh?" he persisted.

"What nonsense! That would mean—
never," she said impatiently. "Biting the
dust! What expressions you use! As if
there was anything to make them bite the
dust!"

"Still, it's a kind of beacon in the distance—a sort of goal to keep in view," he persisted, smiling gently. "So shall we say then, if not before?"

"Oh, if you like!" she said, laughing, but not very joyfully.

"Very good!" he said, with sudden decisiveness in his tones. "Remember, I shall hold you to your word."

"You are not meaning any harm to Brian?" Lucy inquired, with vague distrust.

"Oh, none! I'm only meaning to get the woman I want for my wife as soon as possible. All's fair in love and war." He laughed. "What is Holgate to me— except a stupid bore, without any brains, like all these musical creatures? Feeling —they do everything by feeling—they never reason, by any chance."

"You are not to do him any harm,"

repeated Lucy, trying to speak with a bold carelessness, " or I'll have nothing to say to you."

She meant what she said, and yet at the same time she was glad of something that staved off any nearer talk of her getting married to Dicky Law. It was, as she well knew, a match that would meet with the fullest approval and satisfaction in her home circle, and it was a match which, she supposed, she would sometime or other make. But not just yet—and she did not care to talk about it just yet.

"Why can't you let him alone?" Dicky asked again. "Surely you have got all from him that you want. He's ever so much in love with you—he—— "

" He would go back to the Ormerods if I took no notice of him," said Lucy. " No, I shall not let him alone."

"Go back to the Ormerods—reversion

to the original type," said Dicky, pleasantly. "From the peasantry he sprang, I expect, if the truth were known, and if left to the guidance of his own impulses and instincts, to the peasantry he would return. But we want to keep him raised above such a mere bucolic level as that, don't we?"

"I don't know what you are talking about. I don't understand a word of it," she said crossly.

"Ah, you don't thirst after knowledge. You don't attend university extension lectures, such as we have down in Hollowley," said Dicky, graciously. "It is almost a pity. You might learn a lot at them. And what's more, you might get other ideas into your head than to spend your time tormenting a fellow who is blindly in love with you, and whom you don't mean to have in the end of all."

Lucy looked darkly sulky and annoyed.

She hated to be interfered with and seen through. The game was an important one to her, and she knew that to Dicky it was beneath contempt.

"I can't tell why you wanted to see me," she said, "if it was for nothing but to give me a long lecture like this."

Dicky laughed. "Lecture, indeed! I wonder who gets fewer lectures than you?"

"It isn't for you to begin, then," she retorted angrily.

"Is young Holgate coming here this afternoon?" he inquired, not heeding her vexation.

"I don't know," she answered shortly. "Perhaps he may—perhaps not. Very often Jim and I go and have tea with him on a Sunday afternoon, and then he comes back to supper with us. But I don't think we could take you there, without an invitation," she concluded demurely.

" I guess not. Well, I don't care. We shall meet at the 'Swan' at Hollowley, on Monday night, or else up here again."

" There's the first bell for dinner. I must go and get my things off," said Lucy, turning towards the house.

" What a sweet little prayer-book you have!" he remarked, taking it out of her hand. " And a hymn-book, too, I declare."

" Yes, Jim gave me them."

" Really! If I had had the least idea you had a fancy for such things—— "

" I must not be late. You know father gets furious if any one is a minute behind time for dinner," she said hurriedly, taking her books from him and going quickly in.

" Yes," muttered Dicky to himself, as he watched her light, dainty little figure trip up the slope towards the house; " I know he does. He must have a disgusting big feed, and everybody seated to a minute,

and a full discussion of the dishes, and the
price he paid for each thing, and tell us all
how he never stints his fishmonger or his
butcher as to price, and how well they
serve him in consequence. Bah! What
a place is this, to be sure! What a life for
responsible human beings to lead! Money-
grubbing and eating—that's all they do or
think about; and my young lady there
hasn't even the money-making to keep her
out of other mischief. If she were not so.
d——d pretty with it all! But she is. I
never fought hard for anything before,
unless I was sure it was worth the trouble.
I'm not sure about this at all; at least, not
for the future; it's pleasant enough and
amusing enough in the present. No, I'm
not sure, but I mean to fight for it—and
I mean to marry her if fifty Holgates stood
in the way!"

Then he too went into the house, filled

still with reflections on the life these people led. They all met round the dinner-table; and in such wise had Lucy Barraclough accomplished her usual Sunday morning's occupation—attendance at Divine worship, and then a little stroll round the garden of Jessamine Lawn till dinner-time.

CHAPTER II.

On the Monday night, billiards were re-
sumed, this time at the "Swan" at Hollowley, as Dicky had said; and this time
Brian lost more money than he had won
on the Saturday. He and Jim Barraclough drove home in the latter's dog-cart,
at a late hour; and Brian promised to go
up to Jessamine Lawn on the following
evening, when whist, instead of billiards,
was the form taken by the entertainment.

Brian hardly knew why he had gone to
the "Swan." He had no desire to do so;
he had no wish to play billiards with Dicky
Law; but also, he had no particular attrac-

tion at home.   He felt disinclined for an
evening alone with his violin ; he was too
restless and feverish to enjoy that.   He
might have gone to the farm.   Of course
there was always that resource open to
him.   They never failed to welcome him
and his fiddle.   Perhaps it was partly
because he was so very sure of that welcome that he did not trouble himself to
court it.   But for Lucy, though, he might
have gone.   But he could not sit and talk
to Alice about Lucy, and there was nothing
else now that he cared to talk about.   The
flame of passion had got fresh fuel.   A
few gentle words from her—a look or two,
had roused it all again, and it burnt as
high and as strong as before.   He was
possessed by Lucy and by the thought of
her, to the exclusion of every other object.
Life seemed worth nothing to him till he
had really won her.   And his passion,

while blunting his perceptions in some
directions, rendered them abnormally keen
in others, as is the way with devouring
passions. He had seen, or thought he
had seen, that Law looked at Lucy in a
manner which to him, Brian, was suspicious.
True, Lucy had no manner of interest in
Richard Law. Brian always felt as if Law
and he belonged to different generations
as well as different temperaments, and he
classed Lucy with himself, not with the
other. Still, the bare idea that this man's
eyes could have looked with favour upon
his darling, was enough to set on fire all
his aversion to him. He hated Dicky
with an instinctive hatred, as one hates a
crawling creature, at sight, without waiting
to inquire into any beauty of its own which
it might possess in the shape of wonderful
structure, or minute and curious adaptation
of means to ends; and he hated the very

notion of Lucy having anything to do with this crawling creature. Jim, he knew, was rough and ready, and by no means sensitive as to the company he kept himself, or that was kept by others around him. Barraclough *père* simply did not give the slightest thought to such matters; his days were spent at his works and in his counting-house ; his evenings were devoted to the consumption of a heavy and elaborate supper, and to a subsequent snoozing over his spirits and water by the dining-room fire till bedtime, with occasional pretences of reading the newspaper. If Beelzebub himself had been sitting with his daughter, Mr. Barraclough would have been undisturbed ; for he was not a nervous man. He would not have cared if he had once ascertained that Beelzebub was a sound and increasing character—financially.

Lucy was alone, practically—the only

woman in the comfortless, large house; the
mistress of its servants, with *carte blanche*
to run up bills for household matters, and
even, to a great extent, for her own dress,
if she so chose; but with a very contracted
yearly allowance of pocket-money, a very
limited supply of ready cash for anything
she might require on the spot.   In the
creed of men of the Barraclough calibre, a
girl who had what Lucy had, the use of
a rich father's house and servants and
carriages, required nothing more.   She
was not expected to have individual tastes.

Richard Law knew the exact state of
matters in this respect—so did Brian Holgate.   Dicky perceived in the situation
certain elements possible for him to utilise
to his own great advantage; he had every
intention of some day so utilising them;
and he generally accomplished what he
intended to do.

Brian, on the contrary, beheld a lovely
young goddess whom he adored, and who,
with a coyness or a dignity befitting a
delicately minded young woman, held him
a little at arm's length for a season, until
he should have proved himself worthy of
her.   That was what he meant to do; this
was what he was now setting himself to
accomplish; and the manner in which he
did it was to go night after night to the
abode of the divinity, intending to crave
some private words with her, lay his case
before her, tell her all that he wished to
do, all that he thought he could do; ask
her whether she would rather he made a
name as a great singer, or a great violinist;
or, if her taste inclined to neither of these
paths of glory, would she prefer him to
embark in business, become a prince among
merchants or manufacturers, and for her
sake amass a fortune, not of fame, but of

money ?   All these roads, considered in
the homely freedom of Moor Isles, seemed
easy ones to tread.   It needed but her fiat
to decide him into which of them he should
cast himself, with all the ardour and energy
at his command.   But somehow that fiat
never got spoken ; the question, even,
never got directly put.   He waited his
opportunity ; he had not the faintest notion
that she knew it, and did not intend to
give him one.   It was too serious a matter
to be dashed at without having the assur-
ance of there being plenty of time in which
to discuss it.

And, while waiting this opportunity, there
was always Jim—or Jim and Dicky—to
welcome him. With Jim alone he usually
played billiards, and on these occasions he
saw more of Lucy than when other men
were present. And he seldom lost so
heavily, either, at such times.   When

Dicky Law, and a fourth man, a friend of
Law and Barraclough, were there, they
played whist. It need hardly be said that,
compared with the others, Brian was as a
child, a baby, in his knowledge of the
science of the game. But even these
whist evenings he preferred to the others
—those which were the most frequent—
when he and Jim and Law were alone,
and billiards were voted dull, and whist
could not be played for want of a fourth,
and they sat hour after hour playing poker,
and Brian found that money changed hands
with startling rapidity and unexpectedness.
This kind of thing went on for five nights
out of the seven. Sunday was still exempt ;
and during the autumn and winter season
Brian continued, from old habit, to make
his weekly journey to the concert at Irkford. He persevered in this ; Lucy did
not mind his going there—she minded

nothing, so long as he was not drawn to
the Ormerods. He went, but somehow
the music gradually ceased to have its
former significance and attraction for him ;
never again did he walk home in the dark
with that free, light heart, as on that night
when we first met him, trolling his songs,
filled to overflowing with the joy of the
music and melody, thinking an artist's life
the finest life on earth, and half disposed
to forsake all and plunge into that career.
During the winter there were many more
superb concerts and magnificent singers ;
many a time, from his place in the gallery,
he saw Mrs. Reichardt in her chair down
in the hall; once she caught sight of him,
and gave him a friendly bow and smile.
But the beautiful young girl was gone from
her side—the glorious artist did not that
season reappear at Irkford. All that
episode was over, thrust back, as it were,

obscured by clouds and mists of doubt and
uncertainty.

What was it, he asked himself sometimes, that had come over him, preventing
him from any longer enjoying these things
as of yore? Nothing had happened,
surely; he was the same, he had health
and strength as formerly. Lucy was always
very kind and genial to him, save for a
little coquettish aloofness now and then.
His friends at the farm always had the same
trusting, true-hearted greeting for him;
his dog still loved him; his horse whinnied
with pleasure when it heard his voice or
felt his hand; his old house stood as
before, four-square to all the winds of
heaven, sturdy and abiding, with its solid
gray stone walls, its bonny bit of old-
fashioned garden; the grand prospect from
the front windows of the great sweep of
country, the town of Hollowley, and the

rolling moors beyond. And behind, when he looked forth, behold, as of yore, the sloping green fields with their sheep and cattle; and, rising above them all in the distance, the great dark swell, bleak and wild, heath and bracken clothed, and the square grim head, watching into the north-east, of Ravenside Hill. These things had been his pleasure and sufficement from boyhood—from little childhood. They were all here still, unchanged, and he was here too, and they no longer sufficed him —nay, he was conscious sometimes, when he saw them, of feeling an irritable impatience with them—the kindly, homely faces of man and of nature which loved him, and which he, had he been himself, ought to have loved—they were useless to him. His voice and his fiddle were both more silent than they had formerly been. He often sat brooding, one elbow resting on his knee, while he pulled Ferran's silky ears.

And the only tangible reason which he could give to himself for this change in his spirits was one at which he laughed whenever it crossed his mind—the reason, namely, that he was losing much oftener than winning, in their evenings of billiards, or whist, or poker; that twice lately he had had to draw upon his banking account for money with which to pay the sums he had lost; that this disgusted him, but that, so far from causing him to think of giving up his rational and agreeable amusement, he had got vexedly determined to go on, cost what it might—not to give in to Dicky Law, who was always so confoundedly ready with his little laugh, and his half-sneering suggestion, " Holgate, if we are getting too fast for you, we can stop as soon as you please." Too fast for him,

indeed! Brian muttered indignantly, feeling
all the strength of youth and emulation
and eager desire thrusting him irresistibly
onward. No! He, with Lucy in the
same house, get up and admit that a
bloodless creature like Dicky Law was
"too fast" for Brian Holgate, in any one
way! Never! He would go on; he
meant to go on, if the going should leave
him at last nothing but the roof above
him. "Then I could work; I should have·
to work," he told himself, and went on.

The autumn stole quickly by, and winter
came. The ripeness and richness of Indian
summer were over, the iron-bound sky and
earth of January and February followed.
It was not a joyful winter, if the truth
must be confessed, for several persons at
Thornton-in-Ravenside. It was far from
joyful for Brian, who, filled with passion
and unrest, ambition and resentment, and

teased by the constant tantalizing missing of the thing he most wanted, fancied that to give up the course on which he had embarked would be weakness, and who proved himself truly weak by letting himself be led whither he wished not to go, and made to do things that he despised, and which did not even amuse him. It was not a happy winter for either Alice or her brother, who had to stand by and look on while their hero and their friend grew gradually more and more estranged from them, and more and more dissatisfied with himself. They could see that in his sombre and altered looks; they could only watch it, they could do nothing; and to Alice it was torture even to speak of it. Andrew knew it, and seldom spoke Brian's name to her, and never let her know that he saw the furtive caress she bestowed upon Brian's dog, who, poor fellow, remained unchanged in the midst of all the change about him. The farmer was less reticent; he did not know so much of what was going on in the background, and he often said he was afraid "yon lad" was not so well, nor so well-behaved as he might have been.

It was by no means a happy winter, either, for Lucy Barraclough, who, on the outside, at any rate, appeared to have less care and trouble, of a tangible kind, than. most people. She had never meant that this exploitering of Brian should go so far; it made her unhappy as it took a more definite shape, in the course of weeks and months. She wished to stop it. Had she been, at the end of the winter, as free an agent as she had been on that Sunday morning when she had talked to Dick, after counting the rays emanating from the golden eye above the Ten Commandments,

she would have stopped it. A few words
to Brian, a smile, a private interview, which
she could easily have secured, and in which
she could have hinted her wonder that he
should care to pass his time as he did,
would on the instant have made him strong
as steel against the blandishments of Jim
and Jim's friends. But she could not
venture to speak those words, because she
was in bondage—a bondage which had
been effected partly with her own consent,
and from which she, at any rate, had not
the strength or the courage to break free.
It had been cleverly managed, and easily,
by one who knew her weak points, and
scrupled not to use them.

CHAPTER III.

THE BRACELETS.

AT the beginning of the year, there was a ball in the town, given by the Hollowley Liberal Association, of which organization Mr. Barraclough and Jim were two distinguished ornaments and powerful members, the elder, at any rate, having command of considerable sinews of war. They were not much given to frequenting social gatherings of any kind ; but one must be true to one's party and to one's cause, and the ball came but once a year. Lucy was present at it, of course, looking very bewitching, in a becoming and expensive toilette, and wearing, amongst other

ornaments, a pair of gold bracelets, set
with diamonds and pearls, which had been
her mother's, and which had been not
given, but lent to her by her father, soon
after she had left school. Practically they
were hers ; but not in name. Mr. Barraclough did not love to part with his power
over anything that constituted or repre-
sented money value ; so he "lent" Lucy
the bracelets, and on this particular occasion she wore them.

Law was also of the party at the ball—
not as a dancing man, truly, but to his
own gratification notwithstanding. The
Barracloughs were amongst the earliest to
leave. Lucy did not dare to stay a
moment after her father had informed her
that it was time to go. She looked rue-
fully at her programme, on which stood
half a dozen names against dances not yet
danced. It was so seldom that anything

of this kind came in her way, and she
enjoyed it so thoroughly when it did. But
she was not one of the natures that can
brave blame and brutality; it was easier
and less distressing to fume and obey.
She went into the ladies' dressing-room
to get her wraps, and in a very few minutes
came out again, cloaked and hooded, and
with a changed, uneasy expression on
her face. Law was standing near the
door of the cloak-room, waiting for her.
Her own menkind were not visible at the
moment.

"Are you tired?" asked Dicky, going
up to her, and looking straight into her
troubled face. "Come, and I'll find you
a seat till they come for you."

"No, no!" said she hurriedly. "Come
here, to one side. I want to tell you
something."

She pushed one hand and wrist from

out of the shelter of her fur cloak, and in a frightened whisper said—

"Dick, I've lost my bracelet. What shall I do?"

His eyes flashed a little as she called him in her haste by his Christian name.

"Lost your bracelet? Where, and when?"

"It must have been in that last dance. I never noticed. And then father came and hurried me off. When I was fastening my hood, I saw that it was gone. It is not in there!"—she pointed to the room from which she had just come. "I've looked in every corner. It must have been in the ball-room."

She looked at him with dilated eyes and a pale face.

"What is it like?" he asked her.

"It matches this exactly." She showed him the other bracelet. "They were

mother's, you know. They are not mine.
He only lends me them. If he were to
find out that I had lost it, I don't know
what he would do. You know, he's very
—severe if he gets really vexed."

In other words, Mr. Barraclough, senior,
was in the habit, when exasperated, of
using language that would have disgraced
a navvy, and was capable of even laying
violent hands on—such a person as a
daughter, who could not retaliate. Dicky
was perfectly acquainted with these facts.
He nodded his head gravely, grasping at
once the full bearings of the situation, and
feeling instantly master of it and of her.

"Take off that other one," said he.
"I'll stop behind and have a hunt for the
lost one. Don't look scared, Lucy. You
shall have it back all right. You shall
indeed, if I have to get another like it
made for you. But I guess I shall find it."

She had just time to unfasten it, give it to him, and cover up her arms again, and compose her countenance, when her father appeared, and then Jim. Dicky thrust the bracelet deep into one of his pockets, said good night all round, handed Lucy into the carriage, and saw them drive away, when he returned to the ball-room.

Lucy passed a night and a day of suspense. The evening after the ball, Dicky arrived, and managed to have some words alone with her.

" Well ? " she asked anxiously.

" Well, I'm sorry to say it can't be found."

" Not found ! " she almost gasped. " Dick ! He is just as likely as not to ask to see them. He does, you know, every now and then. Those, and the diamond earrings, and a necklace, and some other things. He likes to calculate how much they would fetch, if he wanted to sell them; and, of course, if one is missing, he is almost certain to ask about them. Oh, heavens! what am I to do?"

"Just do this. If he should ask anything about them soon, say that you damaged the clasp of one of them, and it has gone to be mended; that you confided them to me to see the job through, and you don't know where I have taken them (that's true enough, anyhow), but that it's all right. Naturally, the second one was wanted in order that the broken one might be made exactly like it. See?"

"You are very kind," she said, fully aware how powerful a protection to her was power to say openly that Dick had some hand in the business. There would be no frowns if she could speak up to that effect. "But—but that cannot last for ever—don't you see?"

"No, of course not. But we will have another search for the first one. There are ways and means of tracing stolen goods quietly, and I've no doubt this has been stolen. And I will manage the whole thing for you, if you will leave it to me."

"Oh, thank you! I cannot refuse. And yet—I wonder if he would be very angry if he knew?" she speculated, unwilling to confide so much power to Richard Law, yet dreading with a constitutional dread, at once mental and physical, the prospect of a violent scene with her father.

"Of course he would—mighty wrath, you may be sure. He has not changed his character in the last few days, has he? And it is not suitable for you to have to face any such thing. You may rely upon it that I know what I am talking about. No. Leave it to me; I'll see you through it."

She was silent—and silence gives consent.

A week passed by. Her father so far
had asked no questions. Dicky had not
spoken, and she herself had not spoken.
At the end of the time he came early one
evening to Jessamine Lawn, before Jim
had come in from business. Lucy at the
moment was thinking about the bracelet
and its loss, which worried her incessantly,
and she was wondering (for she had sane
and natural, and even courageous impulses
at times) whether it would do any good
to tell Jim of her disaster, and ask him to
help her out. Then she shook her head.
Jim was not a tender brother. There was
nothing exaggerated or sentimental in his
regard for his sister. " Anything in
reason," he would have said, but the particular request preferred would always
have been out of reason. And, also, Jim

himself was not without some trifling pecuniary difficulties, and his guardian angel, too, in the matter, was Dicky Law. It would not do. She must hear what Mr. Law had to say.

When they were seated together, alone, he produced a piece of tissue paper with something wrapped up in it.

"There!" he remarked kindly. "That's the one you gave me."

"Oh, Dick! And the other?"

"The lost one!" He shook his head. "The lost is not found, by any means—no." He folded his hands and looked at her with an expression speaking of mild sorrow over the circumstance.

"Not found!" echoed Lucy, with a deep, troubled sigh. "Then I may as well tell him about it. I wish I had done it first, instead of leaving it to the last."

"Stop, stop! No such hurry. What should you say to this?"

This time, a beautiful brand-new morocco case emerged from his pocket. Touching the spring, he opened the lid, and behold, reposing on a white satin bed, another bracelet, the exact copy of the one she held in her hand—only brighter and more lustrous ; newer, in fact.

" Dick ! " She could say no more.

" I told you I'd see you through this," said Dicky, in accents of the frankest and most engaging loyalty. " I said, even if I had to have another made like unto the first. There it is. Take it, and make your mind easy."

" Take it—oh, but that is impossible. You have had it made, expressly ? Why, it must have cost a little fortune. You know I have no money but my allowance. I can never hope to pay you for it— never." She hesitated, drew back, did not take it into her hand.

Dicky bent forward and laid the thing, case and all, upon her knee.

" Easily—pay, and more than pay, for it. Some day, Lucy, you'll be my wife, you know—when you can make up your mind to shake off that poor, silly Holgate lad. If I mayn't do a trifling thing like this, to ease the mind of my future wife, and if she mayn't take it, why, it is come to something !"

Lucy looked at him. Truly, Dicky had more chivalry than she had given him credit for. This had all been done in a most romantic, delicate manner, and if her father asked any questions, how easy to show him the two baubles. And if she could not show them—after all this delay —after concealing the loss from him for so long—no, it was quite impossible.

It was impossible—for Lucy.

Yet she felt as if she had been en-

trapped, and that through her own fault.
She could not quite tell where the en-
trapping had come in, or where it was
that she had been off her guard—only
that it had been done.

The conclusion of the scene was that
Lucy did not again reject the morocco
case when it was placed upon her knee ;
that there was a conversation, during which
Law spoke to her more plainly than ever
he had done before ; that at last she
allowed him to put his arm around her
waist and kiss her—that he held her in
his arm for a few minutes, and turned her
face towards him with his hand, and looked
into it with the look of a possessor, saying
all the while the sweetest things about the
privilege of being able to serve her, and
to set her poor little mind at ease ; that
she did not feel the courage and strength
to tell him that he had not set her mind

at ease, but had only transferred the un-
ease from one set of feelings to another ;
that at last, saying she heard Jim coming,
she escaped, and ran to her room, and
slipped the two bracelets into that drawer
of her wardrobe in which she kept such
things; locked it, and then sat down by
her bed and wondered what it all meant,
for one wild moment feeling almost in-
spired to go down again, give that poisoned
thing back to Dicky, confront her father
with the whole story, and—take the con-
sequences.   Some natures would have
acted thus, even at this eleventh hour.
Without entering into psychological reasons,
the fact remains that Lucy's was not such
a nature.   She did not open her wardrobe again, but went downstairs, and said
nothing to her father, who had just come
in, and was grumbling angrily about
something which had gone wrong at "the

works." Dicky looked at her significantly ; she exchanged the glance with a feeble smile ; and in so doing, gave herself over into his power.

Time passed on ; the constant play amongst the men went on ; Lucy felt herself tongue-tied and powerless. Dicky had never made any ungenerous allusion to the little transaction which he had accomplished for her, nor to the money he had expended, in order to give her, as he said, "peace of mind." But the transaction was there—the money had been spent ; the compact entered into. She had no longer the right to oppose an y proceeding of Law's, however wrong she might think it. The bracelet and its history fettered her as effectually as if it had been a pair of handcuffs, and Dicky a police officer, driving her before him. It was a dreary winter. Lucy wondered sometimes how it was that things were so dull, and that she got so little pleasure out of her life. She had worsted the woman whom she considered her rival ; she had one man helplessly at her feet, and another whose chief object in life was to win her ; she was passionately fond of admiration, but her heart was cold and her soul empty. The joy of helpfulness, hopefulness, sacrifice, was unknown to her, and she did not even know what the need was which yet made her whole existence unsatisfactory to her.

CHAPTER IV.

ALICE GOES TO IRKFORD.

ONE fine spring morning, while things of this kind were going on at Moor Isles and at Jessamine Lawn, Alice Ormerod, after despatching her necessary household work with greater rapidity than usual, left her kitchen, which looked spotlessly clean and neat, about half-past eight, and went up-stairs to her room. It appeared that she contemplated some important and unusual expedition, for she speedily divested herself of her print working gown, and took out of her drawers, and from the pegs against the walls, sundry articles of clothing suited for festive or unusual occasions; and she

dressed herself in them. Truth to tell,
when the process was accomplished, and
she had got into her best gown of black
silk and cashmere; her best bonnet of
white straw and black velvet, with some
artificial poppies in it; her best jacket, too,
a handsome enough affair in its way, she
looked, though undeniably a handsome,
somewhat sedate young woman, yet still,
a trifle stiff, and unaccustomed to her
clothes; not so free and graceful as in her
plain, daintily clean prints, moving about,
easy and at home, amongst her farm business and domestic affairs. Still, even in
this trying "best" costume, she was a
noble figure, and her attire did not destroy
the straightforward simplicity of her look
and manner, though they might tone it
down a little.

When she was ready, she went downstairs to the kitchen again. Andrew and

her father were both there. The latter
was somewhat spruced up as to his outer
man : he was going to drive his daughter
in the spring-cart to Hollowley station.

" Eh, lass, art ready ? " he said when he
saw her. " Thou looks rare and well too,
eh, Andy ? "

" Gradely," replied Andy succinctly.

" Are all the things here ? " asked Alice,
bestowing upon each of them a glance full
of affection, if grave and unsmiling. She
had not smiled lately so often as in former
days.

" Let's see," she added, carefully counting
some things ; " the basket with the eggs,
and the pot with the butter, and the jar
with the cream—that's three. Ay, they're
all there ; and my umbrella, and my purse
—yes, in my little bag." She opened a
stout little wash-leather purse, from whose
pockets came the gleam of a goodly store

of glittering yellow coins. "And my
paper, that I've put all the things down
on that we want. And now, father, I'm
ready."

"And so am I," said the farmer. "Come
along, lass; and Andy, do thou tak' care o'
thisel'. Go out a bit this fine mornin',
and don't stop cowerin' in th' ingle o' the
time, while thou'rt fair roasted. Some
day we'st find as thou's got drawn up th'
lover wi' the draught, and we'st ne'er see
thee no more."

"If I once flew up th' lover," said
Andrew, looking rather pleased than otherwise at the prospect, "I should ne'er sit
down again till I found myself lyin' on th'
topmost boulder of Ravenside; and it's the
only way I shall ever get there," he added,
with sudden mournfulness.

His father laughed loudly at the idea,
and Alice, patting his shoulder kindly,

told him, " Those times are all past, lad,
for flying up th' lover, or riding on broom-
sticks o'er Ravenside Hill. Do thou as
father tells thee, and mind thou'rt wide
awake when I come back, that I may tell
thee all I've seen in Irkford, all the time
I'm there."

With that, and a smile of encourage-
ment, she followed the farmer out, carrying in her own hand the jar of cream,
while " Lizzy " followed with the other two
packages. These safely disposed of, and
his daughter seated, Farmer Ormerod
clambered into his place, flicked the whip
about grey Bessie's ears, and with a
lunge, a lurch, and a jolt, they got under
weigh.

It was a lovely morning towards the
end of April ; lovely, that is, as to bright-
ness and clearness of atmosphere, and
brilliant sunshine, but piercingly cold as

to wind, which came piping with bitter
breath from the top of Ravenside, and
was as due north-east as a wind can be.
They had not very much to say to each
other, as they jogged along through the
pleasant lanes of the hill country, passing
many an old grey stone farmhouse, with
its roof of "blue" tiles, or row of curious,
ancient cottages, their cold grey relieved
by the snowy blinds and brilliant masses
of fine flowering plants in the windows.
Gradually they wound down hill, into an
atmosphere less clear and bracing; nearer
civilization perhaps, but most assuredly
nearer to the chimneys and the smoke. Just
before they entered the town of Hollowley,
the rushing of wheels sounded behind
them, and then a high spick-and-span dog-
cart overtook them, flew past them, drawn
by its fast-striding horse, and disappeared
in a little cloud of dust.

"Barraclough's cart," observed the farmer laconically.

" Ay—with Jim and her in it," was all that his daughter replied ; and then, whatever they might have thought, they said no more about it.

At the station Mr. Ormerod pulled up, and Alice got down from the cart. He handed her things to her, but did not get out himself. He had business on hand in the town. He nodded to her.

" Oather I or one o't' lads'll come to fetch thee whoam," he promised her, and flicked his whip again, and drove off.

Alice collected her things and went into the station. It was yet early for the train. They were accustomed to allow plenty of time to drive from Thornton to Hollowley, especially when the catching of a train was in question.

Early though Alice was, however, she

found to her surprise that Lucy Barraclough was already there, waiting apparently for the same train (as a matter of
fact, it had suited Jim's convenience to set
off early, and drop his sister at the station
while he made a call or two in the town
before joining her).

Lucy, too, was dressed for going into
town; so cunningly were her garments
arranged that, though it was absolutely
necessary, in that wind, to wear warm
clothing, she looked like some little hum-
ming bird with brilliantly tinted plumage,
softened down by the rich velvety brown
of her sealskin coat; gleams of colour
appearing here and there at her throat
and in her bonnet. Alice did not lend
herself easily to comparisons with birds or
beasts; she looked exactly what she was—
at a disadvantage with regard to appearance, and perfectly indifferent to that fact.

It was Lucy who accosted the other.
She had no intention of doing anything
more than make Alice uncomfortable, by
saying a few malicious things in a quiet
way ; and the temptation to try that was
too strong to be resisted. Moreover, her
own anxiety on the subject of Brian and
the life he was at present leading, made
her wishful, in a curious, unaccountable
way, to find out what others thought
about it.   .

So she looked at Alice with a placid
smile.

"Good morning, Miss Ormerod," said
she, cheerfully. "We passed you on the
road, I think, didn't we ? "

" Yes," said Alice, unsmilingly.

" Are you going to Irkford ? "

"Yes," again said Alice, who had placed
her three packages on a bench, near to
which Lucy was standing, and who now,

from her far superior height, looked down
upon the other with drooped white eyelids
and scarcely concealed scorn. Lucy saw
it, understood it, realized perfectly what it
all meant, and was furious. Her intention
of amusing herself had gone. What she
now wished to do, was to strike and hurt.
She felt as if she would give the world
to visibly disturb that lofty equanimity of
contempt, that cool disdain of eye and
mouth. They made her feel small—and
that she, Lucy Barraclough, should be
made to feel small by Alice Ormerod, was
an intolerable thing.

"We have been seeing a good deal of a
neighbour of yours lately," she observed,
with a malicious little smile.

"Brian Holgate?" said Alice, after a
perceptible pause, during which she stared
calmly down at the other, and speaking
with unruffled outward calm. "Ay, poor

lad, I know you have. The worse for him!"

Lucy felt as if a sudden ball had struck her. This was her own secret knowledge which she had tried to wrap away from herself in all kinds of sophisms, put into plain, unmistakable, uncompromising vernacular. For the first instant her vivid sense of the truth of the words rendered her silent. In the next arose again the angry feeling that it was intolerable. She gave a light, somewhat falsetto laugh as she answered—

" Heavens ! I had no idea he had given such offence by preferring our society to yours. What harm are we doing to him ?"

" You're teaching him—at least, you've taught him, amongst you—to drink and to gamble, and make a beast of himself. Six months ago, he was a decent lad enough. Now he's more than half-way to the devil.

You and your lot are ruining him as fast as a man can be ruined. That's all."

This heavy artillery somewhat took Lucy's breath away; but though heavy, there was a sting beneath it all, as sharp as a dagger's point—there was the truth, naked and bare. Therefore, being true, it was altogether intolerable that such words should be used.

"Bless me! If he is so decent, and if we are so—indecent" she said, her lips growing pale, while she forced a smile, "how is it that he prefers our company to yours—as I said before? I'm sure nothing could be more decent than your family. They say like seeks like. You've known him longer than we have—why haven't you kept him?"

"Because he's demented just now," replied Alice, with the same sledge-hammer force and directness. "I never said he was perfect—he has his weaknesses, poor lad, and one of them is to believe in the woman he's in love with, and not to understand how false she is, leading him on with promises that she never means to keep, wakening up all his bad passions, and driving away all the good there is in him. You'll hardly say that he has improved since he began to go so much to your house," she added, with imperturbable, calm scorn. "The Scripture says the tender mercies of the wicked are cruel, and it's such tender mercies that Brian is getting just now from you."

"It's easy to see who *is* in love with the young gentleman," said Lucy, forgetting all self-restraint, white with excitement, and with lips quivering with passion. She broke into a little insulting laugh, the eager, raging desire possessing her all the time to make that strong woman wince.

Alice heard her words, and smiled a smile which maddened Lucy.

"Is it?" said she. "Perhaps, Lucy Barraclough, you don't know very well what you're talking about. Brian is my old friend and playmate; we have known each other all our lives. If I found him stripped and lying in the gutter, I'd lift him out and clothe him—yes, if I knew for certain that he would go back to you the next minute, to be stripped again. You don't understand that, of course. I'm sorry for you. I'm sorry a woman can look like you look, and be what you are. And, since you began it, I'm very glad to have had the opportunity of telling you so."

With that, she turned away, looked at the clock, and, seeing what time it was, went into the booking-office to take her ticket. Lucy was left standing, almost panting with anger, with the sense of defeat,

and with detestation for Alice. The conversation had only lasted a few minutes; it had
not been loud, nor attracted any attention.
People who intended going to Irkford by
the coming express were beginning to drop
in and stroll about the platform. Lucy,
after a moment, forced herself to walk
about—forced her face into an expression
of something like composure.

"If he were stripped and lying in the
gutter," she said to herself, or rather, the
words seemed to go whirling round and
round in her mind, so that she could hear
and think of nothing else, "she would
lift him out and clothe him. Very well—I
was sorry, but I'm not now. She shall
never have him in any other way—never—
never! I will teach her what she gets by
treating me in that way."

They travelled in different carriages,
and did not even see each other again.

The Irkford station was crowded. Alice made a porter carry her things to a cab for her. He suggested a "'ansom;" which she declined, with some consternation, and finally drove off in a four-wheeler, having given the man Elisabeth Reichardt's address. She scarcely saw the busy streets through which she was driven—she was thinking, as she had been all along, of that interview with Lucy at the Hollowley station.

" I'm afraid I didn't say what was best for him, poor lad, though it eased my own mind. If I'd known how to disgust her with him, and make her throw him aside— but I'm not clever at such in-and-out ways, and I did hurt her. I meant to. Whatever may happen, she has heard the truth for once in her life—and she knew it was true, too."

But the consciousness of this fact did

not give her unlimited satisfaction. She
was thoughtful, and somewhat depressed,
and scarcely noticed that they had left the
regions of shops and warehouses, and were
now driving along a pleasant thoroughfare,
with trees on either side of it. Then the
cab stopped at the gate of a large, well-
appointed house, standing alone, which
might have been built some fifty years
ago.

"This here's number a hundred," said
the cabman. "Shall I ask if they're at
'ome?"

"Yes, please. Mrs. Reichardt—ask if
Mrs. Reichardt is in."

Mrs. Reichardt was at home, said the
footman who opened the door, and Alice
got out, paid and dismissed her cabman,
and, carrying her different specimens of
country produce, went to the door and
confronted the wondering flunkey.

"I wish to see Mrs. Reichardt," she told him. "She knows who I am. I will give you my name."

"Yes—ma'am," said the man, making a gallant effort to reconcile the homely manner and the numerous bundles with the assured tone and stately beauty of the visitor. And he let her in, and was going to show her into a side room, when a door was opened, and Elisabeth herself emerged from another room, clad in some most wonderful morning gown, all ribbons and lace and frills ; she had a bundle of letters and a newspaper in her hand, and, as a matter of fact, had just finished her breakfast, after being up very late the night before.

She looked, at first carelessly, then with nearer scrutiny, at the figure standing in the hall. Then a sudden light came into her eyes and face—she sprang forward, with hands outstretched, filled as they were with papers.

"Miss Alice Ormerod! no, this is too delightful. You are *most* welcome. You have come on purpose to see me?"

"Well, nearly on purpose to see you," said Alice; and her face, too, suddenly lighted up with a brighter ray than had touched it now for many a week. With all her assured composure in speaking at home of this intended visit, she had had more than one qualm of anxiety lest perchance Mrs. Reichardt, in the multiplicity of her engagements and amusements, should have forgotten her. But she had not forgotten her. She knew her at once, and there was genuine delight and welcome in every word and glance. "Nearly on purpose to see you," she repeated, gladly letting Elisabeth shake her hand in both hers.

"How nice and good of you! Well, come! You will take off your things and stay a long time—all day, if you can. I will send to have your packages put aside."

"They're nothing but a few trifles that I made bold to bring from the farm, hoping you'd not object to keeping them," said Alice, bashfully. "We do have such things fresh and sweet, and I've heard that they don't always in towns."

"Oh, my dear!" cried Elisabeth, her quick emotions touched in the most lively manner, "you are too good. Eggs—why, you must have robbed yourself! Fresh eggs—they are twopence halfpenny apiece here, and called fresh by courtesy. Butter —cream—oh, dear! you make me ashamed to take such valuable things. But I shall do so all the same, and they will be very sweet to my taste, especially because I

haven't in the least deserved them. I
think it is the presents and the pleasures
we don't deserve which delight us so when
they come, don't you? There's a romance
about them which can never attach to the
things we have paid for, in any way.
Robert "—she turned to the footman—
" send Mrs. Lewis here at once, that I
may give these things into her own
hands."

And Alice had the gratification, which
she was by no means of too great a soul
to enjoy, of seeing a stately cook, of critical
aspect, huge girth, and few words, come
sailing into the hall, receive the things,
and, with approving eye and gracious smile,
declare that they were a treat to look
upon. Then Elisabeth took her visitor's
hand.

" Come with me," said she, "and tell me
all that you and "—with a sudden glance—

"Mr. Holgate have been doing since I saw you there."

And at these words Alice's face grew sad again while she followed her hostess upstairs.

CHAPTER V.

ELISABETH LISTENS.

" How often have I thought about you, and remembered your promise to come, and wondered whether you would keep it ! " said Elisabeth, when she had got Alice into her own sitting-room, and made her take off her things, and put her into a very comfortable chair, which, however, rather incommoded the young woman, who was not accustomed to lounges, or lounging, in any shape.

" I thought you might have forgotten me, though I hoped you wouldn't,' said Alice, pleased and soothed, as she looked round the charming room, so full of all

kinds of (to her) mysterious and inex-
plicable things—things which would have
been dreadfully in her way if the room had
been hers. The big writing-table, with its
numberless drawers and pigeon-holes, its
tapers and silver pen-dishes, and piles of
paper and envelopes, and mountains of
papers and notes; it almost made her
head ache, merely to look at them. How
could any mortal woman cope with such
things? The reading-stands, the curious
chairs, the wonderful standing-bookcases,
and others which revolved, the music-
rests, and a hundred other things were
equally bewildering to her. The flowers,
only, she understood. Every glance which
she gave round the room made her feel,
more and more, how utterly different was
this woman from herself, how her life was
filled with interests and amusements which,
to Alice, were merely puzzles. This feature

of the case, taken alone, would have been simply discouraging. But, on the other hand, every glimpse of Elisabeth's own face made it all appear simpler and easier. That was not a puzzle, but a very pleasant and comprehensible fact, and when she looked into it, the room and its mysteries, hinting of spheres of which she knew nothing, dismayed her no longer.

"What a long time it seems since we spent that delightful day at Moor Isles! I have never forgotten that name," said Elisabeth. "At least, it seems a long time to me—perhaps not to you."

"Ay, but it does," said Alice, earnestly. "It's been the longest six months I ever spent. I think time that's full of trouble or disappointment always does seem long."

"I am very sorry if your time has been filled with such disagreeable things," said

Elisabeth. " I remember you saying to me that you would come and see me, even if you were in misery. Perhaps you had a presentiment of trouble ? "

" Perhaps I had," said Alice, sadly. " Anyhow, the trouble's been there."

" Tell me about it, will you not ? " said Elisabeth, gently. " If I can't do anything for you, I can sympathise."

Whereupon Alice did tell her, with a simple, calm confidence and belief in her which touched the tender-hearted woman of the world inexpressibly. Elisabeth listened while Alice related to her all the sad tale of the last six months, not in profuse detail, and in very simple, homely language, but with a power and a directness which made her hearer feel exactly what she had gone through, and yet was going through, of vicarious suffering, for Alice had nothing to relate of her own

home and surroundings that was not bright
and cheerful. Indeed, she remarked casually
while telling her tale, that she did not think
many people had such a father and brother
as hers. She did not tell Elisabeth in so
many words that she was in love with
Brian Holgate, but the love had been part
of her for so long, and her nature was so
transparently truthful, that to one who
knew as much of the circumstances as
Elisabeth did, it was confessed in every
sentence. It was not a tale that seemed
to require comment. Alice did not appear
to have come to ask, " What shall I do ? "
" What do you think ? " of this or the
other. She seemed quite at unity with
herself about it. But it was evident that
she had needed some one to whom simply
to tell the tale, and Elisabeth realized that,
from the girl's very character, she had
come to the person in whom she felt the

most absolute trust, and this fact was balm
to Mrs. Reichardt's soul, and pleased her
more than the most brilliant social success
ever could have done.

Alice did not make a long story of it all;
but, looking into Elisabeth eyes, wound up
by saying—

"It's a sad pity, isn't it, that he should
be so misled?"

"It is, indeed," agreed Elisabeth.

"And now," said Alice, "I want to ask
how you've been yourself all the time since
I saw you, and about the gentleman and
the young lady that came with you to
Moor Isles that day. Has he been in
these parts again?"

"No, he has not. Felix has not been
down here again. He has been very
busy. He always is. He is very popular,
you know, and, what is more, he deserves
his popularity."

"Ay, I liked his face well. I could have trusted him anywhere."

"I have seen him, though he has not been here. I was in London once or twice when he was singing. In the autumn he is going to America."

"To America!" exclaimed Alice, with a sudden look of interest and excitement. "Is he? What for? Is he going to stay there long?"

"For some months, at least. I doñ't know exactly how long. He is going to sing there, of course. He is sure to have no end of engagements when he gets there. They are very anxious to hear him."

"Ay, I dare say. And the young lady —Miss Grey was her name—how is she?"

"Miss Grey is very well, too. She is in London, not at school exactly, but studying

very hard with the lady with whom she
lives. We think we are going to be very
proud of her. She shows a really wonderful gift for the science of languages—what
they call comparative philology—yes, it's a
dreadfully long name, isn't it?" added
Elisabeth, laughing. "Neither Mr. Arkwright nor I understand much about such
abstruse matters, but——"

"I should like to put that name down,"
said Alice, with great simplicity. "I can
never remember it myself, but my brother
Andy will want to know all I've heard
about, and he will know what it means."

"You shall have it," said Elisabeth, with
great glee, seizing upon a little notebook,
and writing the desired expression upon a
leaf, which she tore out, and handed to
Alice. "It means, amongst other things,
the study of very ancient languages ; Latin
and Greek, and what they call the Oriental

languages—the languages of India and
Persia amongst them. We hear she
has an absolute genius for these things,
and Professor Willoughby, under whom
she studies, says that none of the men he
teaches can come anywhere near her. So
she is going to be quite a learned lady—as
full of wisdom as possible, and I think she
will be beautiful too."

"She was very sweet-looking," said
Alice. "Was it true what I heard—that
the gentleman—Mr. Felix, you called him,
has adopted her?"

"Oh yes," said Elisabeth, smiling.
"That was a long time ago. Yes—yes.
She is his adopted—daughter. He is very
fond of her, and she of him."

"I saw that she was very fond of him,"
Alice assented, with some emphasis, so
that Elisabeth could hardly conceal a smile,
as she thought, "Poor Ines! she will have

learnt—already, I dare say, to conceal her feelings rather more than that."

Aloud, she said, " Indeed, she ought to be fond of him.   He has, by his goodness to her, not only saved her from poverty, because there are worse things than poverty—but he has given her a thoroughly happy life, and it is through him that she is now able to follow these studies which she loves so much, and in which she is so likely to excel.   If ever Ines Grey makes a name in the world, it will be because Felix Arkwright put it in her power to do so."

Alice nodded gravely.   "Yes," said she, " I quite see that.   But I don't think that was what made her so fond of him.   It was quite a different expression."

"Well," said Elisabeth, who laughed, and seemed to understand this not very lucid remark, " I cannot tell you anything about that; but I do know that he has been very good to her, and that she repays him with real love and gratitude."

"Ah, yes," said Alice, reflectively. "Do you know what it was made me so take to you that day, and to the others as well? It was because you all seemed so kind and considerate to one another. It seemed to me as if you wanted to do right, and to think right by one another. There was nothing disagreeable anywhere. I thought to myself, well, they are fashionable ladies, and he's a fashionable gentleman, and I've heard that such-like are often so selfish, but I'm sure these have good hearts, however fashionable they may be, and they would be just the same if they were at the very top—kings and queens."

"It was charming of you to see our good qualities so quickly and so plainly," said Elisabeth, laughing; "and in a way

you are right—about Felix, at any rate.
He has been as much flattered, and sought
after, and bowed down to as any prince.
There's no doubt of that.   If you knew
the *idiotic* things that some people do, just
to get him to look at them or speak to
them—women, especially, of course, I'm
sorry to say—if you knew, you would
blush, as I do, sometimes.   And yet, he
has not been a bit spoiled with it all—not
one bit.   Oh, he's a wonderful fellow,
I think, and I'm glad we have been
friends ever since we were boy and girl
together!"

"I don't wonder," said Alice.   "Eh,
how I wish Mr. Brian would have made
up his mind to go from home, and do
something of the same kind.   Not that I
mean," she added quickly, "that he is
great, and a genius like Mr. Felix, but it
would have been something for him to do,

something to keep him out of such-like mischief as he's got into. When did you say he was going to America ?"

"Some time in September, for the winter season there. ' They do everything in winter, over there—in the cities, at any rate."

Alice nodded, and looked thoughtful, and soon afterwards wished to take her leave. Elisabeth, however, insisted on her having some refreshment, and then she departed, saying she had a great deal of household shopping to do in Irkford.

"We only come in about once, or, at most, twice a year," she explained, "and when we do come, there's a lot to do."

With the most cordial assurances and invitations on each side, they parted. Alice had accomplished her wish — she had assured herself that Elisabeth had not forgotten her, or felt less genially to her

than before ; and she had obtained information about Felix and his intended
movements, which interested her.   A half-
formed purpose — more an idea than a
purpose, was already agitating her brain ;
but it was as yet far from being near even
serious consideration.

Meanwhile Elisabeth, left alone for a
few minutes, drew an easy-chair up to her
sitting-room fire, and, throwing herself back
into it, meditated.

"What *is* there," she wondered ex-
tremely within herself, "in that young
man, that should make these two girls be
fighting a deadly fight over him, and with
one another, for his favour ?   For that's
what it comes to.   He seemed to me a
pleasant, mediocre lad enough — rather
good-looking, wasn't he ? yes, blond, with
a bright, open smile; a little boyish-looking
—no particular kind of character, either

one way or the other. There's this noble
Alice Ormerod in love with him, and the
other girl evidently thinks it worth her
while to make an effort to keep him. Is
it mere proximity ? Is it that there's no
one else ? I don't believe that—there are
men enough and to spare, in this division
of the kingdom ! It is not that 'Satan
finds some mischief still,' in Alice's case,
at any rate. It's very odd,"—she shrugged
her shoulders. " I give it up. Of course
he's in love with the wrong woman. They
always are. He is idle enough, as Alice
says. It's a pity. I shall tell Ines about
this visit when I write to her. And I think
I shall tell Felix too—shall I ?—I don't
know, but I should like to tell him that
Alice Ormerod has been to see me, and
what is more, I should like to tell him
what my visitor said about him and Ines.
In my opinion, he is playing with fire in

this experiment of his, and will most likely burn his fingers before he's done.   I hope he will not scorch the little girl to death in the process, that's all."

CHAPTER VI.

MORNING THOUGHTS.

IT was autumn again—October now. The spring and the summer had swiftly rushed by, as time does rush that is speeded with misfortune and disaster. It would be a profitless task to relate in detail how those months had fled. They were over, and the weary story which had begun to be enacted at Moor Isles, at Ormerod's farm, and at Jessamine Lawn, twelve months earlier, was still apparently dragging on. It did not seem to accelerate its pace, but, what was of more importance, its movement, if slow, was always in the same direction—that is, the downfall of Brian

Holgate, once begun, never ceased. He would not, now, have allowed it, even if his enemy had been merciful, and had stayed his hand.

Of course Brian did not call it ruin—he called it standing up with spirit against the man who, he was now quite certain, wished evil to him, and would gladly have seen him, if not absolutely stripped of money and money's worth, yet so reduced that he should no longer be of any account. His fierce dislike of Law, aided by other things, had convinced him that "the fellow," as he always called him, even in his own mind, really was after Lucy. Brian's faith in Lucy was firm, but it had become a passionate effort and endeavour with him to beat Law out of the field, or, at any rate, not to give in—never, never to give in. He was not giving in, but he was getting, if not every day, at least every week, more impoverished in the effort to cope with these two, his companions, as if he were on equal terms with them, in all that goes so far towards success in gambling, as in everything else—in estate, in experience, in capacity for the calculation of chances, in nerve, and *sang-froid*.   He did not take Jim into account; it was nothing to him if he lost to Lucy's brother; but he was embittered beyond description against Law, and resolved to fight it all out to the death.

With regard to his position, he had lost in their continued games of whist and poker, more than one half of his patrimony. His old house remained to him, and rather less than a hundred pounds a year; but he was often straitened for ready money, and his face now never wore any smile.   Lucy's intention, expressed twelve months ago, to find out whether the attractions of the music at Irkford could outweigh that of what she had been pleased to call his "old friends" at Thornton, had been carried out, and the "old friends" had won the day. There were no concerts for Brian this season ; no such healthy, wholesome pleasures drew him to themselves. The spirit which had once revelled in such things seemed to have fled, or been extinguished, and another to have taken its place. The journey which, last year, he had so joyfully undertaken, and the music which had so well repaid him for his pleasant toils, were things that, when he thought of them, seemed to belong to another world. He was gloomy, irritable, or depressed, as the case might be. When he lost money to Jim Barraclough and Dicky Law, and came home cursing his luck, he drank brandy to make him forget his reverses. When, on the other hand, by some unusual

chance, he won from them, he drank more
brandy to celebrate the change in his
fortunes. Everything about him bore the
signs of deterioration, mental and physical.
He was wretched, and he was aware, in
the midst of his own wretchedness, that
he was making others wretched too. He
knew—none better—that it was he who
caused Farmer Ormerod's rugged but
kindly countenance to look stern and hard
when he met him. It was his, Brian's,
present behaviour which brought that sad
look into poor lame Andy's eyes. It was
grieving over his misdoings that had
stamped proud Alice's face with that expression of unshakable sadness. When
she met him now, and said, " Good-day,
Brian," her voice was softer than it had
ever been before in speaking to him, but
it was with the softness born of pity and
sorrowful disapproval ; and her smile, which

she still tried to show him, was so much harder to bear in its mournfulness than an angry frown would have been, that it wrung his very heart to see her, and he would even sneak out of the way to avoid meeting her.

And, what was almost more portentous than any of these things, Sarah Stott, his former tyrant, had become utterly meek and woe-begone. She now never objected to any order he gave, but received it in silence, and carried it out to the letter in lamentation and mourning and woe; almost the more terrible in that it was expressed in no articulate word, but conveyed solely in manner and through a dolorous cast of countenance. He, and he alone, had caused this sad change, had drawn the black cloud over these hitherto smiling skies. There were times when he cared nothing about it. When he was excited—

elated or irritated by gain or loss, he would, if the recollection of this grief that he had caused crossed his mind, shake his head impatiently back, and consign them all to the devil—if they liked to go there. But in the earlier parts of the day—those hours claimed by disagreeable reflection as her own, and which she generally contrives to secure—especially when he awoke in the morning, puzzled and depressed, and when the remembrance of his losses and his woes rushed over him, and his nerves were too unstrung to resist the reproaches of his conscience—at these moments it was that the idea of the suffering he was causing to these faithful, loving souls, was an ache and a stab, a burden which he felt to be greater than he could bear. Then their faces seemed to flit before his mind's eye, and the slow, saddened tones of their voices echoed like a dirge in his ears. Everything in the actual world loomed unnaturally large, vague, and dim in his mind. Only one thing was real—the excitement of the gambling, which had taken absolute possession of him. It had been a gradual growth. At first, as has been said, he disliked the play, and joined it simply in order to be near Lucy. And for some time this endured, the game, when cards were played, being generally whist, in which Law was a proficient. Brian found it stupid; Law found it irritating to play with such an infantile performer as Brian; and one evening, suddenly pushing aside the cards with which they had been playing, he proposed a change.

" Let's have a turn at poker," he said.

" All right," said Jim.

" I don't know it," was Brian's remark. He was indifferent. It was a bore. He knew only that he was heartily sick of whist, for which he had absolutely no taste.

"Oh, we'll soon teach you," said Jim, cordially. "Let's begin now, and we won't have any real stakes till Holgate knows a little where he is. Here's the chips. Shall we suppose it's five shilling ante, eh?"

Law assented, and Brian was forthwith initiated into the mysteries, the charms, the fatal fascinations of draw-poker, and by the end of the evening had grown interested, but had brought no more insight to bear upon the subject than was expressed in his remark when they rose, that it seemed an uncommonly easy game to learn.

"Oh, uncommonly," said Dicky, mildly.

"And it seems to me you can leave off so easily that there's not much risk," added Brian, astutely.

"Yes, of course, you may leave off and lose nothing at all," Jim assented. "Only it's not many who do, somehow."

From that hour Brian was safe and docile in their hands. He could no more resist the attraction of the game than a bird can resist the eye of the snake that is fixed upon it. He lost, he won, he lost again. It soon possessed him; he would lie awake at night thinking over all the chances and possibilities of the game, seeing combinations, or inventing them; realizing where he had been a little incautious, or a shade too cautious here and there; determining to bring his newly-acquired wisdom to bear on the next game, confident that he understood it and its possibilities thoroughly. He was in the net; perhaps he knew it vaguely and in the background, but he had not now the least wish to escape from it. This was reality

–at this a man might make his fortune.
Everything else was phantasmal and un-
stable. It would have been he who would
have raised objections if the other two had
wished to discontinue the play.

And Lucy—he had never yet found his
opportunity of speaking to her, and asking
her what she wished him to make of himself. She was there still ; he saw her often
enough, but never alone. It seemed to
him that she, too, was changed and sub•
dued. Once, soon after the poker era had
set in, it had struck him that perhaps she
might disapprove of his having so thrown
himself into a game so hazardous ; and,
under that idea, he absented himself for
nearly a week from the card-table, but
with the sole result of finding that the
play was almost as difficult to give up as
Lucy was to win, and that its attractions
were rapidly becoming formidable rivals to

hers.   As he did not see Jim and Dicky,
he did not see Lucy, either ; he was filled
with fears and suspicions as to what might
be going on, and he not there.   At the
end of some five or six days, the inaction,
the loss of excitement, the deadly nausea
produced by the effort to think over his
situation, and to take stock of his present
position and future prospects, had reduced
him to a state of nervous depression and
irritability bordering on aberration.   His
existence and his sensations were un-
endurable.   He could think of but one
method of procuring relief for them.

With a plunge, he rushed back again
into the old ways, and in the excitement
of watching his chances, got at least a
temporary fillip to his limp, unstrung
nerves, and forgot, for a season, his actual
position.   He lived, now, in a state of
moral drunkenness, sometimes of physical

drunkenness, too, but of the former always, so that he could no longer discern what were realities and what falsities. His judgment, his nerve, his will, were all weakened, were all getting undermined. What shock would restore the balance, or whether it ever would be restored, who should say? Some temperaments, after their big breakdown, either physical, mental, or moral, recover, and grow stronger, tougher, and more self-sustaining as the years go on. Others, more delicately poised, or of weaker calibre, never recover the original strength—much less do they surpass it in the years that follow the crash. They continue living, moving, looking very much as they used to look, but they are maimed; and if ever they were put to the test, the weak point would show at once.

Brian awoke, one morning in late

October, from a heavy, but far from restful sleep, during which he had tossed and turned, dreamed and groaned, after the fashion of anything but a quiet mind. He had come home very late at night, or rather, very early in the morning, having won, but so little that his gains did not allay the sensations with which he was filled, of rage and bitterness over his persistent "ill-luck;" less capable than ever of admitting that it was not so much want of luck, as want of skill and experience—inferiority to the other players, in fact—that always, nearly, placed him in the position of loser; less capable than ever of giving it up, in consequence, and washing his hands of the whole business. No, he was going to Jessamine Lawn again to-night, of that he was certain, and the same wearisome, tedious, feverish story would be gone through again.

The sensations, both mental and physical, which he experienced in this awakening were horrible. He awoke to darkness. A great black abyss seemed to encompass him round about. Look whither he would, he could see no gleam of light, no cheer, no hope or confidence. It was quite late —after ten in the forenoon, when he awoke, and, after a struggle with himself, managed to rise and dress himself, and to crawl downstairs. Though the sadder season of the year was approaching. this was a lovely, sunshiny morning, mild, still, and genial. The front door stood open, and Ferran lay on the top step, lifted his head at the sound of his master's footfall, rose, and advanced to meet him, with curving motions of love and pleasure, and with affectionately down-drooped head.

Brian, seeing him, and seeing also the sun shining in so pleasantly, went and stood at the open door, the limp tips of his limp fingers just resting on the faithful beast's head. He leaned sideways against the lintel, and looked forth upon the pros-pect, without any care to feign an ex-pression of the ease and contentment that he did not feel. And as he stood thus, Sarah Stott, who had also heard his footstep, came from the kitchen, with a tray in her hands, containing some of his breakfast. The old woman, passing to the dining-room, caught sight of his face, and of its expression. She hastened into the room, set her tray down in haste, and put her hand to her head, suppressing a groan.

"Eh, but it's awful! It fair fleys me to see yon face, and to think as it's our Brian as wears it." She shook her head. All her oracular knowledge, her wise saws and sayings, were here as so much vacant chaff,

powerless to avail aught with him for good
or for evil.

She set the things on the table, and
then came out to him, with a look of
greater composure.

"Mr. Brian, your breakfast's ready for
you."

He nodded, without moving, or looking
at her; but did not look as if he meant
to come in.   She went a little nearer, and
laid her hand upon his arm.   •

"Come, lad!" said she; "come and get
thi' breekfast, and don't stand theer, wi'
that gloppent look—come, Brian, thow'rt
nesh for want o' food."

"I don't care if I never see food again,
Sally," he told her, looking with a dreary
smile into the face of his erstwhile crabbed
and tyrannical servitor.   But he suffered
her to pull him gently into the dining-
room, and dropped listlessly into the chair

she set for him. Sarah Stott retreated into the kitchen, and, hardened old sinner that she was, covered her face with her apron, and wept.

" Eh, my lad ! " she muttered sobbingly ; " eh, my bonny, bonny lad ! To think it should ha' come to this ! What's to be the end of it all ? "

From this attitude she was roused by the appearance, at the door, of the carrier, to know if there was anything to be done in Hollowley.

" Nay," said she, " nowt nobbut to call at Mary Mitchell's on your way back, for th' washin'—that's all."

" Ay ! " said the man, " I have to fetch away Barraclough's washin' too, from there. They've sent a deal o' their things to Mary, lately, and it's a help to her."

Mrs. Stott, whose eyes were by this time perfectly dry, sniffed contemptuously.

"I thought Mary Mitchell professed only to wash for th' gentry," said she.

"Well, Barracloughs reckons to be gentry. They've money enough, choose-how."

"Humph! Gentry! My certy, them gentry!" she laughed scornfully. "*I* saw some of their things one day, when I called in to see Mary. *Cotton towels !*" (No words can paint the withering scorn of her tone.) "A dozen or two of 'em. They have 'em all o'er the house. That's no gentry's habits. You might as well dry yoursel' with a duster ; every bit. There's never been such a thing seen i' *this* house, and never shall, while I manage it ; and we don't set up to be so very grand, noather."

"Well, well," said the carrier, who was a peaceable man, "I'll call for your washin' and tell Mary I'm not to bring no cotton towels along wi' me."

He departed, and Mrs. Stott, somewhat refreshed by this speaking out her mind, went about her work with renewed vigour.

As for Brian, all unconscious of the able championship of his domestic arrangements which was being carried on in the kitchen, he did not remain long at table, nor was there visible much difference in the amount of victual left upon the board when he rose from it. This time, he took his hat from a peg, and, followed by Ferran, went out into the garden, lighted a pipe, and strolled down the steps of the quaint little terraces in which the bit of ground was laid out, till he had descended to the lowest level—a larger space than the rest, planted with fruit-trees and vegetables, and with a number of old-fashioned red and white rose bushes, growing contentedly amongst the gooseberry and currant trees. There he found an elderly man, working with spade and rake, a bundle of weeds lying on the ground near him. He had a pale, somewhat pragmatic aspect, and looked up and nodded as Brian approached.

" Trying to make this old place look decent, Bill ? " said the young man drearily, as he paused for a moment, and removed his pipe from his mouth.

" Ay," was the reply, " and it's none so hard, either. It's been well looked after, has this here old garding."

" Well, I've lost most of my money, Bill. I think this will have to be about the last time you'll have to come."

" Dun yo' mean as I dunnot gardin so as to suit you ? " he asked crossly.

" Nay, nay, but that soon I shan't have money enough to pay you for what you do so well."

" Ah, weel—we con settle that some other toime. Shoo-oo ! "—to a hen which

had found its way over the wall from
Ormerod's, and was now diligently scraping
up a well-ordered bed. "Ay!" he added,
with a kind of slow, sententious chuckle,
as the creature, with much fluttering, fuss,
and clucking, flew back to its proper place,
"yo' can garden so as to suit a man, or
even a woman, though they're a tickle sort
o' fowk to satisfy, but *yo' cannot garden so
as to suit a hen*"—in tones of solemn conviction. "They'll mend it for you, how yo'
mak' it. They can ne'er let well alone."

Brian burst into a short, mirthless laugh,
as he leaned on the wooden gate which
led into a great, bare pasture, sloping for
several acres downhill.

"No, you're about right there," he said
drily.

The man glanced up at him, sideways,
and looked thoughtful. He had known
Brian all his life, and he, too, saw the

changed expression, the haggard eyes, and hollow cheeks.

" Have yo' heerd o' my feyther's travels, Mr. Brian ?" he asked.

" No ; where has he been ? "

" Well, yo' seen, he's near ninety, is my feyther, and he hasn't been so very far afield, all his life. But he were forced to gang down to Hollowley last week, along o' some lawyer's business. He hadn't left Thornton not for nigh on ten years; but he were always uncommon interested in anything he heerd tell of. And he said he mun get his will settled, and he mun have a ride in one o' these here steam-trams. So he did both ; and he coom whoam fair beside hissel ; he were so pleased wi' it all. And he towd us—he says, ' Eh, but them trams are a queer mak',' he says ; ' there's a hecher reawm,' he says, ' and a locher reawm, there is,' says he, ' and th' hecher reawm's a windy spot.'* B' the mass! we laffed at him—we did so!"

Brian again laughed, rather drearily. The time had been when he would have chatted with the man, drawing him out, and hearing all kinds of quaint, old-world lore and expressions, hearing the words used which are to be found in the " Faërie Queene," and which are to this day vernacular in this district, and in no other part of England. He used to delight in such little talks. But not to-day. He moved on, nodding to Bill, and wishing him a brief good morning, and then he went back towards the house. The man looked after him, with a shrewd, commiserating expression.

" In a bad way !" he said to himself, and went on with his weeding.

* "There's a higher place, and a lower place, and the higher place is a windy spot "—*i.e.*, draughty, cold.

Many hours lay before Brian ere the business of the evening could begin—the question was how to get through with them. Nowadays, when he had once opened his eyes in the morning, from his heavy, yet unrefreshing sleep—when he had once aroused from the wild dreams which pursued him, and showed the depraved state into which his nerves had got —no feeling of rest or repose, no momentary drowsiness, even, ever came to his aid during the long day. It had to be lived through, and endured with full, over-clear consciousness ; every moment to be, as it were, reckoned with. The daylight hours had become a long torture to Brian, and, having once arrived at that condition of mind, there was little wonder if he looked forward with a hungry longing to the evening, when at any rate there would be excitement to drown the thoughts which had accumulated, black and dreary, during the day.

This morning, going into the house again, he wandered for a time, aimlessly, from one room to another, and at last, coming to a standstill in the larger parlour, his eyes fell on yesterday's newspaper, lying still folded, on the top of the piano. It was one of the large Irkford papers, and he picked it up, more in absence of mind than anything else, and casting himself into an easy-chair, opened it, and glanced over it. The first page contained, as usual, announcements of all the amusements—concerts, theatres, public meetings, religious gatherings, circuses, free-thought lectures, etc. Conspicuous amongst them was the advertisement of the coming concert.

"Mr. Frank Warburton's grand concerts. To-morrow" (that, he reminded

himself listlessly, now meant to-day) " Mr.
Felix will sing 'The Sapling Oak,' and
the aria from Marschner's opera, ' Hans
Heiling.'—' *An jenem Tag' da du mir*
Treu' versprochen.' "

" Lord, what a distance off it all seems,"
thought Brian, bitterly and wearily.
" What's to hinder me from going to the
concert to-night, as I used to do ? I'm not
so weak in body yet nor so poverty-stricken
in purse, that I couldn't manage that." .

But though he did not admit it to
himself, but continued to dally aimlessly
with the idea of going to Irkford, yet the
fact remained that he had no longer the
power of will to accomplish such a breaking loose from the present state of things.
In his heart he knew well enough that he
would not go to the concert ; but would,
after getting through the day as best he
could, and when night had set in, go up to

Jessamine Lawn, and there resume the now nightly occupation.

Then he opened the broadsheet, idly still, and on the middle page saw a paragraph headed, " Approaching departure of Mr. Felix for America." There followed the information that to-morrow's concert afforded the last opportunity which the English public would for some time enjoy of hearing their favourite artist, as Mr. Felix sailed on Saturday from Liverpool for New York, in the Cunarder, *Batavia*, with the intention of making a prolonged stay in America, and of singing in all the principal cities of the United States and Canada. He would remain in Irkford until the Saturday morning, when, accompanied by friends, he would leave for Liverpool, and sail at 2 P.M. The sole manager and agent for Mr. Felix during his American tour, it was added, was Mr.

Charles Percival, who accompanied him, and it was requested that any inquiries or communications might be made to him at such and such an address, and by letter only.

Brian read this paragraph with suddenly roused interest and attention; then threw the paper down and reflected upon the matter. He was in no mood to do justice to others, or to see his own or any one else's circumstances in a true light, and he bitterly and angrily asked himself what he had done that there should be so great a difference between his lot and that of this other man. Felix himself had spoken in the highest terms of the quality of Brian's voice, and had said that had he only begun an artist's career early enough, he might have ranked with the very first of them. Felix had his voice and nothing else— Brian had an absolute genius for that most

difficult and delicate of instruments, the
violin. Felix, again, had started on his
career with scarce an advantage—his father
was, and always had been a poor man; had
failed disastrously in his brief attempt to
cope with business men on their own
ground; had thankfully retired into ob-
scurity and lived there since, a learned,
unworldly scholar, existing on some three
hundred pounds a year. Felix had succeeded; none but himself knew how hard,
how unflinchingly he had had to set his
shoulder to the wheel; how many inborn
likes and dislikes he had smothered or
silenced in order to gain that success.
Brian had begun life with more than old
Mr. Arkwright's income assured to him,
ample funds on which to live while he
studied and worked. He had had no in-
cumbrances, no dependents, no poor relations to drag him down—nothing but

himself and his own advantage to consider. Yet here was the one man a world-famous artist, whose smallest doings and movements were chronicled like those of royalty, and whose exercise of his art procured for him just as much money as he chose to ask for. Moreover, in him, as Brian had observed (with delight and admiration then, with sour envy and bitterness now), there was a strong, self-reliant independence of outside things, a cheerful, sane, and healthy way of looking at life and of taking things as they came, which added to the charm he exercised over those with whom he came in contact.

"I dare say," Brian muttered angrily to himself, "I should feel cheerful and independent if I were like him—a sort of king, with all the world at his feet, and men envying him and women worshipping him. Ah, if I were like that, Lucy would not hold out any longer ! I should be sure of her, the only thing I care for, and—ay, there's no rhyme or reason in it—why one man should have everything and another nothing."

At this instant Mrs. Stott entered the room, with floury hands and with a cooking-apron covering her gown.

"Eh, Mr. Brian, are you theer? Mesther Ormerod's sent across to ask if you'd lend him yesterday's newspaper for an hour or two. There's summat as he wants to see in it."

"Ay, there it is," said Brian, pointing to it as it lay on the floor. " He's welcome, and he can keep it. I've done with it."

" Why not tak' it across thisel', lad? It's long enough sin' thou were theer. They'll be fain to see thee,".she said coaxingly.

He shook his head with vexation.

" Nay, give it to the servant, or whoever it is," he said shortly.

And poor old Sarah, not wishing to irritate him (she who had never hesitated to speak her mind to him as plainly as if he had been her own child), took the paper and left the room with a sigh.

Farmer Ormerod found what he wanted in the *Irkford Chronicle;* it contained every week an excellent article, entitled " Farm Notes," treating of butter-making, cattle rearing, silage, sweet and sour, and the best methods of preserving it, with other matters appertaining to the mysteries of farming life, and the good man studied it and laid it down.

That same evening, just about the time at which Brian's steps turned towards Jessamine Lawn, Alice Ormerod, wearied with a hard day's work—she worked very hard now, with a sort of insatiate fury

for employment not natural to her well-
balanced organization—seated herself in the
ingle, having exhausted every task she
could find ; and she also picked up the
newspaper, and, after looking over it at
first indifferently, she likewise appeared to
find something which interested her, for
she read attentively for some time and
then sat and gazed into the fire, unconscious
of the scorching of her face and eyes ; and
the thought in her heart as she shook her
head sadly and sternly was—

" Eh, if only that could have been ! "

CHAPTER VII.

DESPITE the rural solitude in which Jessamine Lawn was situated, and the engaging
innocence of its name, very late hours were
constantly kept there—hours which were
whiled away in anything but innocent
employments. It was seldom that the
party of card or billiard players separated
before the small hours, by which time Mr.
Barraclough the elder would have been
for some hours in his bed, and Lucy, too,
would have sought her couch ; or, at any
rate, her room, whether she slumbered or
not. Then, when they at last gave up,
Brian would pass his hand over his fore-

head, hot and burning with the excitement of the play, and would try to bring
himself back again into the actual present,
while the others, paper and pencil in hand,
made out the reckonings. He generally
went away with one of thèse little accounts
in his pocket, containing a business-like
statement of his losses—rarely of his gains
—which account he was free to contem-
plate on the following morning; free, also,
to speculate upon the best means of
procuring the necessary amount, if he did
not happen to have it in the house. He
always brought it up with him on the
following evening, when a peaceful settle-
ment took place all round, losers paying
up like men, and winners pocketing their
gains with the easy grace of conquerors;
and then, all scores being cleared, they
were free to start afresh, "with easy
minds," as Jim affably observed.

It so happened that on this particular evening the proceedings were not destined to be carried on as late as usual, as will be related. It also so happened that Brian had no occasion to take with him either gold, notes, or cheques, as he had gone away the night before slightly the winner. But, as has been related, he went in an evil frame of mind and a shattered condition of nerves, down on his luck, suspicious and jealous, and passionately anxious to worst Law, and beat him out of the field.

The three of them sat down about nine o'clock to the usual poker. Brian's brief run of luck of the evening before seemed to have deserted him, and he still trusted to luck, never having fairly grasped the adage which Law had so often uttered, namely, that " cards, in poker, are nothing compared to knowing what to do with them when you've got them."   Brian's

hands were wretchedly bad, and he felt
his irritation rising as one after another
was dealt to him, each one, as it seemed,
worse than the last. He failed to note
that the others were very little better off
than he was. The betting was not ex-
citing; the pools were small, and were
taken now by Law, now by Jim, but never
by Brian. They played on for more than
an hour; there was nothing to presage a
storm, or the occurrence of anything remarkable, and Brian began to realize that
amusements are sometimes as hard work
as the treadmill. He was sick of it, and
would gladly have given up, but that would
have been too ignominious. It was a
lesson to find that the wild game of poker
could sink into a miserable inanity, no
more interesting than would have been the
measuring out yards of ribbon over a
counter. Jim was saturnine, Dicky imper-

turbable, as usual. Law was watching Brian quietly the whole time, and the first change in the state of things at last took place when the deal happened to be Brian's. His chance, it seemed to him, had now arrived. He found that he had dealt himself three kings, a three, and a four.

He could no more have helped the change that came over his countenance, incautious though it was to give the slightest sign, than he could have flown. He raised his head, and, with an excited look, said—

"Here goes! I'll make good my ante, and five pounds better. Who's for playing?"

Dicky, after one imperceptible glance around, saw the raise without the slightest change of expression. Jim, whose cards were worth absolutely nothing, threw them down.

"I'm out," he observed.

"So it's between you and me," said Dicky, with his gentle smile. "Well, I haven't much to boast of, but I'll see you through, anyhow. I'll take one card, if you please."

Jim raised his eyebrows at the apparent artless candour of this admission, but spoke not. Brian gave a card to Law, and dealt two to himself, retaining his kings, and discarding his three and four. The cards he drew were nothing less than two aces, giving him a "Full," not to be beaten by anything less than "Fours."

"Humph!" said Dicky, quietly; "threes, I suppose, and you beg for a full, but I've seen you do that before."

"He means it this time," said Jim, carelessly. "Keep your hand steady, Holgate."

"You mind your own business," said

Brian, in sudden irritation, and shaken by the excitement of it—" you haven't paid either to play or to criticise!"   Then, turning to Dicky, he added, " It's no good, whatever you get—you had better pass over the pool and let us start fresh."

" Thanks for your good advice.   Let's get on with the game.   I bet five pounds."

" See the five, and ten better."

" See the ten, and five better."

" See the five, and fifty better," said Brian, frowning and going rather pale.

" Oh, here's a high old bluff!" muttered Jim, who was looking on with extreme interest.

Brian did not notice him.   Dicky, appearing not to notice anything, took up his cards, which were laid before him, and examined them carefully, as if to be sure he had fallen into no error.   Then, half to himself—

" It's robbery—I've half a mind to see the fifty, and stop it." He darted a quick glance from under his half-closed lids at Brian, and after the lapse of a second or two, " See your fifty, and five better."

" See your five, and a hundred pounds better," followed quick as thought from Brian.

" Holloa, Holgate! are you aware that it will cost me a hundred to go on ? "

" Yes, I am. Put up your hundred, and as much better as you like."

" Humph! See the hundred, and five better."

" I say," observed Jim, " I call this getting too stiff. I'd drop it, if I were you."

" It's not for me to drop it," retorted Law, calmly. " My raises are only five pounds. It's the most I dare do."

" See your five, and five hundred better,"

said Brian, also calmly, but not with the calm of an easy mind.

"Oh, Lord!" said Jim, in his own mind. "What must such a fellow play poker for —he shows every change in his face, like a girl when you pay her compliments. He's got a big hand, too, to go on like this."

"I suppose you know what you are doing," said Dicky, deliberately. "Because I know where I am; and if you're simply bluffing, remember, I can last longer than you can."

("By George! What does he mean, talking in that way?" was Jim's inward comment.)

There was an angry flash in Brian's eye, as he answered, "I'm going to do as I please in this game, without your advice or any one else's."

He knew that if Law had fours, it must

have been dealt to him, since he had only begged one card—and he knew, too, that the chances against such a thing were about four thousand to one. He would push it on to the bitter end. And he looked wrathfully at his opponent; while Jim, again within the recesses of his own mind, said to himself, "Good Lord! it's like playing with a baby!"

"As you like," said Law. "It's my turn to bet. I believe you have six hundred and eighty on now. I'll make it seven hundred to oblige you. So it will cost you twenty pounds to play."

"I'll see it through," said Brian. "What do you call Moor Isles worth?"

"Moor Isles—what do you mean?" came from both the others.

"What I say. What value would you stake against it?"

"This is absurd," said Law.

"Told you I would do as I pleased," said Brian, doggedly. " Name the amount you think it is worth, and stake against it, or pass over the stakes to me."

" Moor Isles is worth—from seven hundred and fifty to a thousand pounds," said Law, slowly.

" Say a thousand," Brian remarked.

" Well, a thousand—and if you stake it, it may stand as a thousand pounds staked. *If* you will do it. You had better consider."

Brian, perfectly oblivious, in his excitement, of the fact that Law could at any moment stop the game, and that he never did, but each time dexterously "raised" his opponent, said—

" It's twenty pounds to play this time. There's my note for Moor Isles. See your twenty, and a thousand better."

" That means," said Law, as if reflecting,

and warning Brian at the same time, "that I can see your hand if I make good the thousand."

"Yes, that is it," said Brian; and his breath seemed to fail him. The game was his—that Law had no such cards as his own, he was convinced. This victory would compensate for all the previous defeats he had sustained.

"It will cost me a thousand pounds to see your hand," said Dick, pensively. "Well, see your thousand, and one thousand better! Now it will cost you a thousand to see mine!"

Brian saw on the instant how he had been befooled. Because Law had raised five and ten pounds steadily throughout the game, he had decided that he would continue raising five and ten pounds. He had intended to "see" Law this time, and show his hand. There was no question of

any such thing now.   He had not the fifth
part of a thousand pounds left in the world.
He could not pay what was necessary to
enable him to see Law's hand.   Law, who
so quietly went a thousand better, had any
number of thousands more with which to
continue his game.   Brian knew that he
was entrapped, beaten, ruined.

"I can't see that," he said, and laid his
cards down.   The cards, the table, and the
forms of his companions swam before his
eyes.   It was only with a mighty effort,
resulting from his almost insane determina-
tion not to give in before Law, that he at
last pulled himself together again, and
heard Dicky's voice, saying quietly—

"I take the pool."

"It seems so," said Brian, mechanically,
staring from one to the other of them, and
feeling as if he were still in a nightmare.
The strain had been horrible.

Jim, when Brian's haggard eyes rested upon his face, withdrew his, and looked at the table, the cards, the chips—at anything.

"Would you like another game?" asked Dicky, civilly.

"No—unless you like to play on—for love," said Brian, with a grim little laugh.

"Not much fun in that," was Jim's somewhat embarrassed contribution to the conversation. "No, I vote we stop for to-night, and to-morrow Holgate can think about it, and see how he stands. We should be sorry to lose him."

"Oh, very," said Dicky, politely. "But it might be as well for him to stop for a bit. He doesn't look well, and you ought to be up to the mark all round, to get any enjoyment out of poker."

These were the only words by which Law expressed any triumph over his ruined opponent, but they were more than enough.

Brian stood up, and walked away from the table.   Jim, leaning over to his friend, asked in a low voice—

"What the devil did you hold?"

Dicky looked at him quietly.   "I asked Holgate a thousand pounds to see my hand, and he wouldn't.   Do you think you are going to see it for nothing?"

And he shuffled his five cards into the pack.

"I don't mind about staying any longer," said Brian, from the other end of the room. "I'll go back—to Moor Isles.   I wonder if Lucy is up yet?   I'll say good night to her if she is.   Perhaps it may be a long time before I see her again."

"I don't know," began Jim, with a look of sheepishness and hang-doggishness combined.   "It's after eleven, you know, and—— "

"Oh, I guess she won't have gone yet,"

said Dicky, cheerfully, and with an appearance of the greatest candour. "As you
say, Holgate, why not say good night to
her now ? Come along, Jim."

But just at this juncture, before Brian
could inform them that he wanted none of
their company in the interview he was
seeking, the door was opened, and Lucy
herself looked into the room, as she occasionally did, before going to bed. At first
her face wore a slight smile, and her eyes
travelled involuntarily in the direction of
the card-table. Then a look of surprise
crossed her countenance at the unexpected
vision of the three men standing, with
anything but undisturbed expressions, instead of being, as usual, seated, silent and
intent, round the card-table. She missed
the customary rapid upward glance of
Brian at her entrance—a glance which, in
spite of her double-dealing, she felt the

want of, and to which she unconsciously
looked forward.

"What! Have you done already?"
she began, and came a little forward into
the room, for, truth to tell, she was glad
of a little company of any kind in these
latter days, and the prospect of half an
hour's chat, even with these three men,
every one of whom bored her no little in
reality, presented itself as a pleasanter
alternative than finishing her lonely evening by going to her lonely room, and lying
awake for several hours, wishing that Brian
Holgate would go. Despite her resolve
to punish Alice Ormerod through Brian,
Lucy had no desire to punish Brian himself; she was sincerely uneasy about his
present conduct, and she had become
wakeful of late. The thing had got on to
her nerves, and she had acquired the bad
habit of listening and watching, not for

some one to come, as is often the case
with women, who can only wait, cannot
do, but for some one to go ; before she
could slumber—and the effects of a mid-
night waking are very much the same,
from whatever cause it may arise.

"Yes, we're quite good and virtuous,"
Dicky answered, as the other two made
no reply to her. "We have finished for
to-night, and were just about to part
company."

Lucy began both to feel and look uneasy. She misliked it ever, when Dicky
spoke in that genial, satisfied tone, as if he
were an innocent, open-hearted creature
who wished well to all the world, and
could not imagine that any one could
possibly wish any evil to him. Reasoning
from the known to the unknown, she looked
quickly at Brian, and could not understand
the import of his expression. He was pale

—he had been pale for a long time now. He did not look excited—his eyes were cast down, and he was smiling a little, in a peculiar way which she did not like. Dicky was smiling and pleasant. Jim, her brother, did not seem altogether at his ease; as it seemed to Lucy, he did not look quite satisfied with everything. And there was something in the air, as it were, which filled her with uneasiness, though they were all three apparently so quiet and collected.

Certainty may be considered by some strong natures preferable to suspense, but the impulse which suddenly took possession of Lucy with overwhelming force was to get away from this scene—to leave it and these three silent men to wind up their accounts alone. She did not want to know what the something was that lay behind it all. She felt as if she would much rather not know it; and, acting on this impulse, she said—

"Oh, well, then I won't come in. It's after eleven—time for all decent people to be in their beds; so I'll wish you good night."

"Stop one moment, Lucy," said Brian, in a low voice—he spoke rather quickly too—that was the only sign he showed of any excitement or agitation. "I've something to say to you. Perhaps I shall not see you again for a long time. I need not take up time with telling you why. My friends here will explain that afterwards." (Dicky nodded as if to say, "Ay, I will, old fellow." Jim wriggled uncomfortably.) "Anyhow, that's the truth. I'm forced to go away from here, and it may be long before I come back. So I wanted to say good-bye to you, and to tell you——"

"Why, Brian, what should make you

want to go away?" she interrupted, her woman's instinct discerning at once what kind of words he was intending to say to her, heedless of the presence of the other two, who, indeed, did not at this moment exist for Brian, in the almost savage joy he felt at finding the barriers at last broken down which, invisible and intangible though they were, had yet all this time prevented him from speaking out to Lucy as effectually as if they had been composed of triple plates of steel. It was strange, though it never struck him, that for months he had been waiting to see her alone, and win her over to him, and had allowed all kinds of small obstacles to prevent the interview, and now he felt the strength and the power to set everything and every one else aside, and say just what had been burning in his heart, and eating it out for so long.

And Lucy knew this; she saw in an instant what he meant to say, and a great fear took possession of her, so that she felt as if she would rather die than hear what he was bent upon uttering. But her feeble effort to stave it aside was futile. This time it was he, not she, who was strong and who ordered how things should go.

"Why should I want to go—because I'm ruined!" he answered, without any hurry or bluster, but with a calm that was much worse than all the ranting and raging ever indulged in by ruined man. "I'm ruined; stripped naked and bare—not in law, I suppose, but in honour." (Lucy stood still; the words were like a horrible echo of the conversation she had had with Dicky more than a year ago.) "And it has all happened for your sake, Lucy; not that I want to blame you," he added hastily, as he saw a sudden expression of terror

come over her face. "Oh no! You are
not to blame; and, for your sake, I don't
grudge it. A man must take his chances,
I suppose, and to win you it is only right
that he should work very hard and have
something to offer you worth your accept-
ing. And so long as I had the means of
getting near you without working, do you
see, it was too strong for me. I couldn't
tear myself away. Now I shall be obliged
to. There's nothing else for it, and I
don't mind. I'm young and I'm strong,
and I can get on well enough when there's
nothing to keep me back. And you won't
mind waiting, I know. It won't be for
long, and if it were, you would be the
same to me if you were old and withered
as you are now, never doubt that, Lucy."
His voice sank into a tone of the deepest
tenderness, and his face took an almost
rapt expression, so that poor, passionate,

vacillating Brian Holgate looked beautiful
with an almost unearthly beauty through
the expression which lit the eyes and
suffused the countenance worn with excitement and with the furious mental wear
and tear of the last twelve months. He
advanced towards her, holding out his
hand.

Lucy stood white and speechless before
him, feeling that the long-accumulating
results of the game she had been playing
had now gathered themselves together,
and that there was no escape from them.
If she had been alone with him, she might
have abased herself and explained, or she
might have cajoled and deceived him once
again. As it was she was utterly powerless, defenceless, and while listening with
hot cheeks to Brian's passionate words,
could all the while only hope, in a feeble,
helpless kind of fashion, that Dicky would,

out of his distaste for scenes of any kind,
let the farce be played out without telling
Brian the pitiless truth.   It all depended
on his good pleasure.   Now she saw to
what an extent she had placed herself in
his hands.   Until she had got a word or
a sign from him she was paralyzed and
tongue-tied.

Brian had literally forgotten the other
two.   It was Law's voice which once more
awakened him to the fact of their presence.

"Lucy," said the master of the situation,
coming round and standing beside her,
"you may see that Holgate is a good deal
excited.   We'll hope things are not so bad
with him as he's disposed to think, and in
the mean time, as he seems to be under
some little mistake about your feelings for
him, we had better have a proper explana-
tion.   It is best to face facts always; I
think he does best to go away, and it's

quite natural he should wish to say good-
bye to you. You're old friends, and I
understand all that. But it would be a
pity to let him go away under a false
impression about either of us; therefore,
we may as well tell him that most likely
when he comes back, he'll find Lucy Barraclough has become Lucy Law—eh? Do
you see, Holgate? Lucy and I are
engaged to one another, though we have
not cared to say anything about it; and I
see she is not inclined to talk about it
much, even now. Ladies often do not like
to have a fuss made about these things.
Still," he added soothingly to her, "you
need not look as if you were going to
faint, Lucy," and he supported her with his
arm, for in very truth she looked as if she
could not stand.

"Keep your hands off her, you dog!"
said Brian, looking at him, his eyes blazing

scornfully from his pale face while he stood and looked at them both, and became, if possible, each moment more white, more wrathful, and more despairing-looking. "No doubt you'd like well enough to have her. Do you think I've never seen that all this time? But she isn't going to be entrapped by you in that way. Engaged to you, you pitiful, lying sneak! If she weren't here I'd give you the name you deserve!" He laughed unpleasantly.

All this, it must be remembered, was taking place very quietly. The voices were not raised; the gestures were not excited of any of them. It was not a brawl, but a life-and-death grapple, and any one outside passing the closed door would have heard nothing more than the ordinary tones of an ordinary conversation. Brian turned to Lucy once more, and his voice melted into all the music it was capable of, and that was a great deal.

"Nay, Lucy," he said, "come to me— don't fancy I will ever let him touch you" —though it was Law's arm which at this moment kept her from falling—"come here and tell me he lies—not that I need to hear it, but just to settle him."

"Yes, tell him I lie, Lucy," said Dicky to her, with a calm undisturbed by Brian's low-toned, passionate invective. He held her more firmly in his arm, and Brian, for all his brave words, stood there and did not fell him to the ground.

"Tell him, Lucy," said Dicky again. "Do I lie, or do I speak the truth?"

"Speak, Lucy!" said Brian, after another pause; "it's you who have got to settle this thing now. He says you have pro- mised to marry him. I say it's a lie. Is it a lie, or is it not?"

"No!" came in a whisper from Lucy's lips, but in a whisper which was audible enough to all those who heard it.

"It's best to face facts," said Brian, a sudden sharp, cruel look crossing his face —the kind of look which can come into the kindliest eyes, the sort of feeling which can overmaster the sweetest natures under certain combinations of circumstances. It was as much the instinct to preserve himself and not own that he was beaten, as any desire to torture her, which prompted his next words.

"Best to face facts. So you have lied to me?"

No answer.

"You have tricked me and duped me."

Silence.

"You have known what was going on here, and you have sat by and never said a word."

Still she did not speak.

"And all the time you knew I was coming here for your sake, and you were letting him make love to you, and knew all that was going on—you were letting him do as he pleased with me."

There was another pause. Dicky whispered something into Lucy's ear to the effect that she must not mind—Holgate was mad with defeat—it would all pass over. Brian meantime walked close up to them and said to her—

"Lucy!"

She looked up. What she felt was that she hated them all, and would have liked to make them every one suffer what she was suffering now.

"You've done this," he said, smiling; "you are no better than a ——."

Lucy shuddered as the shameful epithet struck her ears. Brian went on in the same deliberate way—

" It's just the same sort of thing that the worst girl on the streets would do. Some of them wouldn't. They would have some pity. A man may be very sorry for that sort of girl, but he doesn't want to marry her ; at least, I don't. It seems there's one ready to take you, so I'll leave you to him and wish you good night ! "

Dicky's arm was powerless to support Lucy any longer. She writhed out of his clasp and sank in a terrified, sobbing heap against a chair which stood near. Horrible, horrible words ! Could a woman ever get over such a shame ? And what, oh, what had she ever done to deserve that such words should be addressed to her ? Was ever a girl more cruelly and undeservedly ill-used than she had been ? And that it should have been said to her before these two other men ! She suddenly sprang up, made two steps to her brother, seized his arm, and, in a panting voice, cried—

"Jim, you coward! you coward! How dare you let him say it? It's your fault, and *yours!*" she turned with maddened eyes towards Law; "and you let *me* bear the punishment!"

"I say," said Jim, turning to Brian, "you'd better look out what you are saying to my sister, or it will be the worse for you."

"Your sister is worthy of her brother, and does honour to him; and her lover and your friend is the exact match of you both," replied Brian, with a sneering laugh, as he walked towards the door. "No doubt it seems all right to you, but some people have a way of thinking that the sort of thing you've been doing is not what honest men and women do. You can easily judge whether the cap fits."

With that he closed the door and left the house, leaving them to consider his words.

CHAPTER VIII.

ELISABETH IS DISAPPOINTED.

On the Friday morning, the day after that scene at Jessamine Lawn, Elisabeth Reichardt and Felix Arkwright sat together in her house, over, it must be confessed, an inordinately late breakfast. There had been a supper party the night before, at the house of one of their musical friends, and to-night Elisabeth was having a farewell reception for her friend at her own house. Perhaps neither of the good souls had the courage to face the prospect of a quiet evening *tête-à-tête*, with the parting of the morrow standing before them. Old

Mr. Reichardt, who had, in good old German fashion, had his *Frühstück*, literally his "early bit," long ago, and had, ever since, been diligently employed in the perusal of his English and German newspapers, had greeted them as they came down one after the other with some little jest about the late hours they kept; had talked over last night's concert, and congratulated Felix on his rendering of a certain song of Schumann's, which was a great favourite with the old gentleman; and now he rose to make his usual excursion into town, to hear the news of the business in which he no longer took an active part—to call at his club and see the latest telegrams, and incidentally to collect a little gossip and furnish himself with an appetite for lunch. He said a friendly "Auf wiedersehen" to them and took his departure, leaving them alone.

There was silence for a time between them, as they proceeded with their meal. Elisabeth smiled to herself every now and then. Felix was rather grave, and drank his tea and consumed his fish in a business-like manner. At last Elisabeth, with a certain look of effort, said—

"And do you actually mean, my good friend, that you are going away without a word or a sign to the little one?"

Felix looked up, and the expression that crossed his face showed that this topic had been discussed between them before, and that he was now reminded of it—not altogether pleasantly.

"I told you so, Lisa, didn't I?"

"Yes; but I didn't believe you. It was just after your arrival—just when you were hurrying off to rehearsal, and I supposed you had not time to add the qualifying clause."

"There is no qualifying clause. I meant what I said."

"I still cannot believe it. I cannot imagine you doing anything so—so un-comfortable for me."

He smiled slightly. "I know you have a great confidence in your own power of getting just what you wish for, and that the confidence is, as a rule, well-founded. But if you wish for this, why, disappoint-ment awaits you. And I don't see exactly why it should make *you* uncomfortable."

"It makes me vicariously uncomfortable. I suffer for Ines."

"Quite unnecessary. Ines knows nothing about it."

"You imagine that they don't read the newspapers at Madame Prénat's?" she said, with withering emphasis. "I can tell you they do, even though they may be printed by steam, and full of lies."

" Well ? "

"And do you suppose Ines ever takes one up without looking through it to see if your name figures in it ? "

" If she ever was guilty of such folly, let us hope that a year's experience has cured her of it."

He spoke rather coldly, and looked as if he would prefer to change the subject. Elisabeth, however, had had this topic on her mind for some time. She had chosen this method of opening it out, as it were, and she intended to go on with it at all risks. But, intimately though she knew Felix Arkwright, his character and disposition, privileged friend and confidante though she was, she still felt a little trepidation as she went on—

" A year's experience of what, Felix ? "

" Of the fact that she can get on very well without me, and that there are other people in the world quite as interesting as I am—which was what I intended her to learn."

"Well, you know, I call that rather assuming things to have happened, while really knowing nothing about it. How do you know that the year's experience may not have had just the opposite effect?"

"Not likely," was the brief reply.

"Nothing more likely," retorted his friend decidedly. "Remember, I have seen her since you have. I called, as I told you, the last time I was in town, and had her to dine with me at my hotel. I saw nothing to show that she was in the least changed. Felix, I'm going to say something to you which I know you will resent —at least, I'm afraid so. If you don't like the thing, you must look to the motive that prompts it. You are going away for a long time, and to such an immense

distance, that I should hate to have anything not quite clear and plain between us.
Do you see ? "

He nodded, but did not look altogether
pleased as he threw one arm over the back
of his chair, and, instead of looking at her,
fixed his eyes upon the fork with which
his other hand trifled. Elisabeth leaned
forward, her elbows on the table, her hands
clasped, and looked earnestly at him.

" You know," said she, " that I have
never asked you why you took that particular course with Ines a year ago. I felt
you did not care to talk about it ; I felt it
would be presumptuous in me to approach
it ; but, Felix, you know, as well as I know
—your looks have told me many a time
that you understood me when I looked at
you—you know, I repeat, that that girl
is in love with you."

She had spoken, and her steady look

did not reveal the nervousness she felt.
For a single instant the hand of Felix,
which was balancing the fork on one of its
fingers, shook ; the fork fell upon the
table. He pushed it away from him, looked
directly at Elisabeth, and replied gravely—

" I know that a child of seventeen, with
a lively fancy and an exaggerated sense
of gratitude for what I have done for her,
may have unconsciously allowed herself to
think a little too much about me. Since
you speak about it, I can—to you—not
to any one else. She had not the cunning
or the experience to hide it. She was
over-grateful, poor little thing ! It is not
a weakness one often meets with. Such
things will happen, I suppose, now and
then ; but if they are taken in hand in time,
no harm comes of them ; and I took it in
hand in time."

Mrs. Reichardt sat listening to this dis-

course with an indescribable expression on
her face.   It was not laughter; it was not
sadness ; it was not mockery ; perhaps it
contained a little of all three of these
things.

"Since you say you will speak of it to
me," she said gently—"which I appreciate
in you as a mark of confidence—tell me
exactly how you took it in hand, and what
effects you expect to follow from your
course of action."   .

"I took it in hand by committing her
into Madame Prénat's charge, and explain-
ing to that lady that I wished Ines to
'come out,' in a certain sense ; and I decided not to see her again for a couple of
years.   Two years between seventeen and
nineteen will make as much difference in
her as twenty, or at any rate, ten, would,
when people get to our age, Lisa."

"Still both under forty, my good sir ;

not at all too old to have susceptibilities
and emotions of many kinds. However,
I now understand you better; you admit,
though reluctantly, the fact that I urge.
I am not much surprised at that. And
you did not wish to make a fuss about it,
to hurt her feelings, or to lay bare her
secret to any one else—in that you were
right, and I like you for doing it. Whether
what you have done will have the effect
you anticipate, that's another thing altogether. *Par exemple*, why not have let
her come to visit me now and then?"

"Because I thought it best for the
separation to be complete—that's all."

"H'm! One can't always cure a bad
habit by one single effort of will. And
you told Madame to take her out a good
deal? Why, I wonder?"

"Because I know the society Madame
frequents is beyond all suspicion—it is

very good society; you know that—neither
the fast and fashionable, nor the out-
rageously rich and vulgar. I felt that if
she met any one under Madame's wing,
and fell in love with him, and he with her,
it would be certain to be all right."

"You take my breath away. Talk of
women being such trusting creatures! But
I see your motives; they are excellent.
And suppose she goes out and meets
people, and does not fall in love with any
one else?"

He shrugged his shoulders.

"If so, it cannot be helped. She could
have no better home than with Madame
Prénat; with her she shall remain. She
will learn that I am her friend and well-
wisher always. And it is not as if she
had no brains. Ines will never die of
ennui, especially in that house."

"But," Elisabeth persisted, gently but

firmly, "suppose she not only does not fall in love with any one else, but does continue to be in love with you?"

"I wish you would not speak in that way—making a child's passing fancy into a serious thing. She will not do anything of the kind."

She shook her head, with the same look of mingled sweetness and bitterness of feeling. A man—the kindest-hearted of men—even her friend Felix, dealing single-handed with the mystery of a girl's heart, —it filled Elisabeth with wonder, with pity, and with a little mournful amusement also.

"Ah, well, let a man get into his head the idea of a system," said she, "and when facts go against that system, so much the worse for the facts! Stay, Felix," she added, seeing a look approaching to anger in his face, "don't mind that. I think it is awfully good of you to have endured this

catechism from me; but one thing more.
You may say what you please, but it is
possible that things might turn out in that
way; she might only have grown fonder
in absence, you know.   Hers is not a fickle
nature ; and at nineteen Ines Grey will be
as beautiful a girl as you or any one else
could wish to see."

"Well ?"

"You say you mean to see her again at
the end of the time.   That may be wise, in
you, or it may not.   But do you mean that,
supposing that were the case which I have
imagined possible, you would not marry
her yourself?"

" No, I should not marry her myself."

"Do you mean that you would let some
false notion about difference in age, or
taking advantage of her, or something
quixotic of that kind, step in and spoil
your happiness ?"

Felix was silent for a time, looking down at the table, with an expression Elisabeth could not understand. She watched him in some anxiety. The idea of the possibility of this marriage had haunted her, as a kind of pleasant dream. It had delighted her; she had pondered over it many a time, though she had never before spoken of it. She wondered now at her own audacity in going so far; but the matter—especially the matter of the happiness or unhappiness of Ines Grey— was one which lay very near to her heart. What did that look of Felix mean? What would he say? She was prepared to fight to the death any scruples he might entertain, of the kind she had mentioned. At last he looked at her.

" Not in the least, my dear Lisa. I am not such a paragon as you seem to think me. I feel quite sure that if I wanted to marry her, I should perceive dozens of reasons for doing so, and should be vastly hurt and offended at her ingratitude if she did not see her way to complying with my wish; but—my dear woman, don't look at me in that horror-struck, reproachful way —I don't want to marry her. I never shall want to marry her. I'm not in love with her, if you will kindly try to believe me. She is a sweet child; it would be impossible to find a sweeter child anywhere. Many a time I have congratulated myself that she was *my* sweet child, and from the very nature of the case a child she will always remain to me." (Elisabeth, with almost superhuman self-control, refrained from retorting, "For all that, she failed to see nothing but a father in you." She had her ends to gain and was silent.) "I could spend weeks with her, and thoroughly enjoy her company and her cleverness and her dainty ways, and be glad she is so pretty—I like beautiful things—but my pulse would never beat faster for the tenth of a minute all the time, nor should I ever feel hotter or colder for her proximity or her absence. When I parted from her— you will think me a brute, but it is the plain and simple truth—it was because I saw that, in her enthusiasm, she ran a danger of being somewhat unhappy about me, and as I had not the least intention of being unhappy about her, it seemed to me in the highest degree unkind to—— "

" Put danger in her way. Well, I have courted this disclosure. I have brought it on myself, and it serves me right. I don't know whether it is what I might have expected, or not, but I could cry—yes, I could cry, with disappointment ! "

" I'm very sorry, but what can I do ? "

" Nothing. You are always so horribly

sane and clear and certain in all your views and intentions. I could scold you—oh, how I could scold you! So like a man, to begin a romance and never finish it. As for Ines, my heart bleeds to think of her."

She rested her chin on her hands, and tears actually did rise to her eyes, and burnt there, though they did not overflow. She had spoken rather too plainly, in her chagrin.

"Your heart bleeds for her? I am sure I don't know why," he said in a tone of extreme vexation. "Surely there would have been more cause for it to bleed if I had played fast and loose with the child. I haven't. I have acted as straitly by her as if—— "

"It's difficult to find a parallel case," she said, laughing vexedly.

"You can surely give me credit—— " he began.

"Oh yes, yes; you have behaved like a *man* and a gentleman, Felix." (Was there a touch of raillery in the words, "like a *man*"?) "Under the circumstances, I suppose there was nothing else for you to do. And I am sure you have been very patient, and you must be left to carry out your own experiment to the end. But one hates to be put in the wrong, and have one's hopes dashed to the ground. Thank Heaven, Ines herself suspects none of this."

Here her footman came into the room with an envelope on a waiter, and went to Felix.

"A telegram for you, sir. Will there be any answer?"

He tore it open, and read it. There was a moment's pause. Then—

"Well, of all the nuisances that could have happened—no, no answer. Read that, Lisa," and he gave it to her as the man left the room.

It was before the days of " sixpenny wires," and the message ran—

" Mrs. Lauriston, Birmingham, to Mr. Arkwright, Queen Street, Irkford. My son very ill typhoid. Must give up journey. Great regret."

" Why, that is your companion that was to be, isn't it—young Lauriston ? "

" Of course it is. My go-between, factotum, *âme damnée*, everything. Percival is no good in anything but the barest business matters. And a good fellow too. I counted on him absolutely. By Jove, but I'm sorry for this ! They are very poor, you know, and the lad is a hard-working lad. His salary was evidently a great object to him, and I meant to have given him many a hint about his voice, and how to begin his career. I am sorry."

" I shall inquire into it," said Elisabeth, promptly. "Why must they go and be living in Birmingham? I wonder how soon he would be fit to go out to you, if you could get a substitute in the mean-time?"

"Oh, I suppose I could go on, some-how, without any one; but it is such a frightful bore having either to see people— people who sometimes make such asses of themselves—or to say you won't see them. And he really understood about it, and he liked me, too; and I am sure I liked him. It was worth anything to see his delight at the prospect of seeing the world under my auspices. Well, typhoid is typhoid. The unlucky young beggar, to go and get it just now !"

There was a perturbed silence; Felix flicking the telegram impatiently to and fro, Elisabeth thinking profoundly.

"*Must* he be a gentleman by birth and education ?" she asked.

Felix laughed. "Well, I should prefer it, I must say. I know what you are thinking of," he added, looking severely at her rather conscious face. "One of your beloved Reedley's *protégés*. I dare say he could find half a dozen who would be willing to go, but I want help, not hindrance."

"You had better take Ines—such a child, and yet she would be a help," said Elisabeth, sweetly and maliciously. "Or give up the undertaking altogether."

"No, I mean to go through with this. If they think it worth their while over there to pay to hear me, in their usual style, I shall be almost at the end of my road by the time I get back. Besides, I want to see the Great Republic."

Elisabeth shook her head. It was no

secret to her, though it remained a mystery, that Felix Arkwright was not in love with his profession, though he might be with his art. She had at her command all those worldly goods for a portion of which he was working, and she sometimes wondered what he would say if she told him she would like to divide them with him—and remain free. But the immediate question was, not his feelings about his profession, but the means by which to find him a substitute for the secretary and companion who had been taken ill in so untimely a manner.

And at this juncture the footman again made his appearance.

"There's a young person, ma'am, who says you know her, and she is very anxious to see Mr. Arkwright. I was to say her name was Ormerod, and her business was very important."

"Alice Ormerod!" cried Elisabeth. " She wished to see Mr. Arkwright ?"

"Yes, ma'am.   I've taken her into the library."

" What does this mean ?   Felix, come !"

They went out of the room together.

CHAPTER IX.

ELISABETH DISAPPROVES.

ALICE was indeed waiting in the library, but still standing up, where the footman had left her. Her face, though calm in expression, was very pale, and there was something in her eyes and on her mouth telling of mental suffering—severe suffering. Elisabeth saw it at once, and at once said to herself, "The young man has been behaving badly; but what can she want with Felix?" Felix saw it too; but what he felt was that this young woman was not at all like the young woman he remembered seeing at Moor Isles, and that, either from ill health or some other cause, her beauty was much diminished. That was his first feeling.

"Alice Ormerod, I'm glad to see you," said Elisabeth, heartily, as she shook her hand. "What brings you here, though?" And then, seeing a sudden pained look cross the other's face, she quickly added, "But never mind. I'm glad you have come. My servant said you asked for Mr. Arkwright. Here he is!"

"I made so bold," Alice answered, in a trembling voice, as her eyes timidly and for a moment rested on Felix's face. She had fancied that she remembered him so vividly and exactly, that he was the most approachable person she had ever known, and that it would be so easy to speak to him. But now, as she stood face to face with him, under these different circumstances, and saw how gravely he looked at her, she suddenly felt him very formid-

able and imposing ; and as the nature of
her errand flashed through her mind, and
the recollection that these two persons,
kindly, well-meaning, were perfectly in
ignorance of what brought her there, they
seemed to swim before her eyes, and for
a moment her courage failed. But only
for a moment. Straight and outspoken
she had been born ; so she would live, so
she would die. And after one moment,
during which she met the steady gaze of
Felix with an equally steady one of her
own, and felt as if a wave of a cold sea
had passed over her, she was herself again.

"It was in the newspaper that I saw
Mr. Arkwright was here," she said—"at
least, that he was in Irkford; and I thought
he might be staying with you. It's the
greatest chance that I ever found it out.
It's the greatest wonder that things should
have happened just as they have, and I

hope neither he nor you will think me very impudent if I asked to speak to him alone—if he has the time, that is. It's a matter of great importance to me, at any rate—and to some others," she added, with a sigh.

Elisabeth had been holding her hand and looking at her all this time, and she now turned to Felix and looked at him.

"You can spare the time, Felix, can't you?" she asked; and he saw that she very much wished him to say yes, despite the smile in her eyes which she could not quite repress. There was something so artless in Alice's simplicity, that if they had not both realized by now that she was in great distress, the smile would have appeared on their faces, as well as in their eyes.

"I wonder what in the world she can have come for?" Felix speculated. "But

I suppose I shall hear what she has to say. It's rather a miscellaneous programme, this, just before setting off."

And aloud he said, "Yes, certainly, I can give Miss Ormerod a little time, if her business is urgent."

"I'll make it as short as I can," said Alice, humbly.

"Then I will leave you," said Elisabeth, turning away.

"Look here, Lisa," he said hurriedly, "don't utilise the opportunity to send for half a dozen candidates for Harry Lauriston's place; do you understand?"

"*I* understand," she replied, in a tone more of sorrow than of anger, as she shook her head; and saying to Alice, "I shall see you again before you go," she left them.

"Won't you sit down?" said Felix, pushing forward a chair, and looking attentively at the girl. Her cheeks were a little flushed now, and he saw her strong and simple beauty assert itself once more. And her distress, so bravely battled with, moved him.

"Thank you," said she, "but I don't know whether I can sit still to tell you what has happened."

Nevertheless, she did sit down, and clasped her hands, from which she had taken the gloves—the unwelcome restraint necessitated by a journey to Irkford.

"You remember, sir, I expect, the day that you and the two ladies came over to Moor Isles, and had dinner and tea with Mr. Brian?"

"Perfectly," he said. He, too, had seated himself beside a table, on which he rested his elbow as he faced her.

"I thought you wouldn't have forgotten, for all you have so many engagements

and so many friends. Eh, sir, but poor
Mr. Brian did think a deal of you! He
was never tired of talking about you."

"Did!" echoed Felix, startled. "You
speak as if he were dead."

"Oh no, no! He's alive, thank God——
And yet," she added quickly, raising her
clasped hands together, and then letting
them fall again into her lap, "I don't know
why I should say, 'thank God!' I think
it would have hurt me less to see him in his
grave than brought so low as he is now."

No tears came into her eyes as she
looked at him, but an expression infinitely
more sad than tears overspread her whole
face.

"I suppose I am to do something or
other for that lad," Felix said within himself. "There's some great mess taken
place, I can see. Then aloud, but encouragingly—

" I am very sorry if any misfortune has happened to him. What is it ? "

" You are very kind," said she, almost breaking down at his tone of interest. " Perhaps you'll remember, too, that before you left that evening, a young man and his sister came in, and sat down to table, and had tea with you ? "

" Yes, I remember that too, very well."

" Well, sir, all Mr. Brian's friends were sorry he had so much to do with that family. They are not a good family. There's bad blood in them. They're not true, and they are not honest, and their friends are like themselves. Oh, never believe that it was his nature, of himself, to have gone with such people. It was because he had fallen in love with her. If she had been true and honest it would have been all right, whatever the others might have been ; but she was like the rest of them—false. They do say you could never depend on a Barraclough, man or woman, keeping their word. Even if it went against their own interests, sometimes, it seemed as if they had to be false. She was false. She played him up and down, and led him on, and wouldn't say yes or no, and let him keep coming to the house, and made him believe she was going to take him some time or other, and all the time she was promised to another man—one that had a power over her; and this man and her brother just set to work, and took advantage of his love for her to make him play cards and billiards, and things I don't understand—nor he either, poor lad! They wanted him out of the way, and to ruin him was the only plan that came into their minds. Well, he wasn't strong enough to lead that kind of a life, and he got quite mad—quite, quite mad. Mr. Brian hasn't been in his right mind this many a week."

She paused, and choked down some kind of a sob, while Felix sat and listened, and wondered what it was all leading to. Somehow it did not sound as if it were going to be an appeal for money; but what, then, could it be? She went on by-and-by.

"It had to come to an end at last, that kind of thing. He went up there last night, and as he doesn't generally come in till nearly morning, Mrs. Stott—that's his old servant—was surprised when she heard him open the door before twelve o'clock. She had gone to bed, but she heard him come in, and go into one of the sitting-rooms; and then she heard him groan, and then all was quiet. She was frightened—too frightened to go down; but she never shut her eyes to sleep, you may be certain,

and she got up very early, between four
and five in the morning, and went downstairs, and, though she was very frightened,
she went into the parlour, and there she
found that he had never gone to bed, but
was thrown down in an armchair, just as
he'd come in; and he was sleeping, and
groaning in his sleep, and Ferran, his dog,
had his nose on his knee, and was looking
up into his face most pitifully. She didn't
dare to waken him up, but she stepped
across, and told me and my father; and we
went to his house—we were sure there
was something very wrong. And they
said that I'd better go in and awaken him.
Mrs. Stott thought he might be angry
with her, if he saw her first thing. So I
went into the room; but he had just opened
his eyes, and when he looked at me, I do
think, for half a minute, he didn't know
me. And then he says, 'Why, Alice,

what time o' day is it? Have I been
asleep?' And then he saw the lamp, and
that it wasn't daylight, and he sat up, and
looked about him, and at me, and shuddered. I just said Mrs. Stott had been
afraid he was ill, and had sent for me, and
I said didn't he think he'd better go to
bed, and try to get a little sleep. He
only laughed at that, and then—oh, sir, I
thought my heart would ha' broken—it all
came back to him, and he said suddenly,
' Alice, I'm going away from here, and I
must tell you what's happened, that some
one may know what has become of me.'
And then he told me how they had played,
and played, and betted so high, he said;
I'm sure I don't know what he means, but
at last he got desperate, hoping to beat this
man—Law, his name is—and he staked the
very house that he lives in—Moor Isles, sir,
that he loves better than anything in this

world, except the woman that's brought
him to this—and he lost it.   That sobered
him, I know.   But as if that wasn't enough,
he went to say good-bye to her, and then
this other man, who has no more pity than
a tiger, and who wanted to get him out of
the way for once and all, turns round
upon her, and forced her to confess that
she had ever so long been engaged to be
his wife. Ay, it seems impossible that
such wickedness can be ; but what I tell
you is every word true." (And, indeed,
Felix did not doubt a syllable of her story.)
" He told me all this, and then he said
death was much better than life for such
a fool as he had been, and he was going
away—he didn't know where—over the
moors, or anywhere, and perhaps he might
die if he stayed away long enough."

Again she paused.

" And you ? " asked Felix.   " Why did

he choose you to tell all this to—about his love for this other girl, and all the rest of it ? "

For a moment, but only for a moment, her face flushed painfully. She was past any coyness of concealment.

" I hope, because he knew he could trust me in anything, and ask anything from me," she said. " I'm his oldest friend. We were playfellows together when we were little children; and we were like brother and sister when we were boy and girl; and since we've grown up I've hoped for nothing so much as his happiness. And he has always been true to me—as his friend. That is why he told me."

" And you have come to tell it all to me —why ? " he asked, not unkindly, but almost reverentially.

" Yes, sir; I came to you, not because I've any claim upon you at all, but because

I trusted you when I first saw you, and knew that you had a kind heart, and were true. When Mr. Brian had got a little quieter, but before I'd called the others in, he said to me again, ' Eh, Alice, where can I go to be furthest away from all this ? If I could put fifty thousand miles between me and Thornton, I think I could even wish to live again.' Well, a sudden thought came into my mind. I said to him that he must bear up, and have patience for a day, and I thought perhaps I could manage for him to go a long way off, if it wasn't fifty thousand miles. I'd read in the paper the day before all about what you were going to do. Mr. Brian thought all the world of you, sir, and I've just come to tell you all about it, and ask if you'd let him go with you."

Felix stared at her for a moment.

" Let him go with me ! " he at last ejacu-

lated, and then, silent again from excess of
astonishment, once more sat and gazed at
her. He had had a good many experiences
of different kinds during his career, but not
one quite like this, and he began to wonder
whether he had not heard wrongly.

Alice, however, soon set him right on
that point.

"Yes, let him go with you," she repeated
resolutely, as she looked at him earnestly.
" He must go away, or else he'll either
kill himself, or something bad will happen
between him and those two men that have
fleeced him so. He can't go alone—at
least, it would be a very bad thing for him
to go alone. He can't hire any one to go
with him—he has played away too much
of his money for that. But he won't be
dependent on your charity, sir, either.
He has told me all that has happened, and
there is something left—just because he

wasn't able to get at it in a minute ; and
we'll see to that.   We want to save him."
(She spoke as if it were all settled and
arranged. Felix could not guess how
suffocatingly her heart was beating.) "He'd
be proud to go anywhere with you, and
I'm sure he might be able to do something
or other to help you.   At first he may be
a little sad and low, but he'll remember
what is due to you.   And you mustn't
think," she added, with almost painful
earnestness, "that because he has been
gambling with these men, and has nearly
ruined himself, that he's fond of low company.   No ; he never was.   He never did
like drinking or anything bad, till he fell
in love with a bad woman. Such a woman's
place ought to be amongst other bad
women," Alice went on, with remorseless
outspokenness, "and not in what people
think is a respectab'e house, where every-

thing seems as if it was what it ought to be. That's what has ruined him—not love of bad company. He'll do nothing to disgrace you ; I can answer for that. And now you know everything, and it's in your power and in your hands to save him, body and soul, if you'll undertake to do it."

"To save him, body and soul." As she ceased speaking, these words echoed in Felix's ears. A noble task, no doubt, he thought, hardly able to repress a smile, as the humour of the situation, of whose very existence Alice was unconscious in her earnestness, presented itself to his mind. The only thing was, he was not a missionary, given over to the saving of reckless, passionate young men's souls and bodies ; and he felt very little inclination to turn missionary in this particular case. The idea of setting off on his tour accompanied by the blighted young man brood-

ing over his blasted hopes and perfidious
love, was by no means a pleasant one to
him. He would feel him a responsibility,
and a frightful bore—this last was what
Felix most keenly felt—a bore—such a
bore as had perhaps rarely fallen to the lot
of mortal man. He did not suppose that
Brian, accustomed to be his own master,
lead his own life, consult himself alone as
to his actions, would be of the slightest
use to him in the capacity of useful companion. No ; if he undertook the thing
it would have to be without any hope of
reward, save the proverbial one rendered
by virtue to itself. If he undertook it, it
would be—his eyes again searched Alice's
face, and he felt it very keenly—it would
be because he was too soft-hearted to send
this young woman away with, so to speak,
her confidence betrayed, her purpose, which
was pure and unselfish, frustrated, and her

hopes disappointed. With what an effort
she must have strung herself up to seek
this interview and ask this favour! She
had put on an undaunted front, but Felix
knew that it must have cost her a
tremendous struggle to go through with it.
In hope, in trust, in the fervour of love and
self-sacrifice she had come; her errand was
to send away the man she loved—to let
him go now, away from her—not selfishly
to keep him near her, and make use of the
revulsion which the other woman's deceit
might have produced in his mind. What
would she feel if she had to return with all
her passionate endeavour fruitless, so much
eager effort useless? What a dreariness
there would be—what a hopelessness over
those two houses this night! As this
aspect of the case came strongly into his
mind, there came also the feeling, un-
defined, but convincing, that he would not

send her away empty-handed and aching-hearted. She was a brave creature, he said to himself, a simple, true-hearted woman. In Felix's own character there was, perhaps, something of the same generous, uncomplicated simplicity of feeling and action ; but as a man of the world he felt that it would not do to make unreserved, unconditional promises.

" I don't know about saving him," said he. " People generally have to save themselves, you know. But, supposing I were to consent, do you think he would come ? "

" Yes ; I can answer for it—he would."

" I will tell you—it is a singular coincidence—that I have this morning had a message to say that the gentleman who was going out with me to help me in various ways, is ill with fever, and has to give up the journey. Now, I cannot take a useless person with me. I want some

assistance from my companion; he would
have to write letters, see people, and make
himself useful in various ways. Do you
suppose that your friend, in his present
condition of mind, and accustomed to consult no one but himself as to what he will
or will not do, would be able or willing to
submit to orders, and perhaps give up his
own wishes for my convenience—for that
is what it comes to when one person agrees
to make himself useful to another."

"I'll put him on his honour," said Alice
promptly; "and I'm certain the bare idea
of getting away, and having something
quite different to do and to think about
from what he's ever had before, will be
the saving of him. Besides, he does think
a deal of you, as I told you. It's been
clouded over lately, but it will come out
again when he's free from what has been
making him so mad."

Felix bowed gravely, thinking within himself that to be held in such high esteem was not always the most convenient thing in the world. But he had swiftly made up his mind to do what this young woman wanted him to do, and he was not going to spoil the concession by making it ungraciously.

"Well," he said slowly, but not unkindly, "you know him—or, at any rate, you ought to know him and his character well. You speak as if you understood him, and I am sure you have his welfare at heart. I liked the lad very much, I must say, when I met him, and I am truly sorry he has fallen into such bad hands. I think I will do as you wish, Miss Ormerod—with this reservation," he added, raising his hand quickly, as she was about to speak—"that I do not by any means pledge myself to take charge of him or even to keep him in my immediate party all the time I am away, or under all circumstances. You will excuse me if I speak plainly, and remind you that I am going abroad in a public capacity, not a private one. I am bound to fulfil my engagements to the public, whatever may be the state of my private affairs; and should I find at any time that young Holgate caused me trouble, or in any way interfered with my arrangements, I should feel myself perfectly at liberty to tell him that we must part company, and that he must rely upon himself and his own resources. You understand me, I dare say?"

"Yes, indeed, sir, I do; and he will understand too. Oh, sir, there's things that one person can do for another that no thanks can pay for—nothing but our lives can show we are grateful; and you are doing such a thing for me now, and for him, and for all of us, to-day. And——"

She made a sudden pause. The colour rushed over her face, the tears to her eyes. She looked at him in affright, and half whispered, " Eh, I seem as if I only just knew what I'd done. What must you have thought of me ? "

For the first time during the interview she saw him, not as a strong abstract power, able to get her what she wanted, but as a man, a very human man—a man with whom she had been pleading desperately for the man whom she loved; and it suddenly rushed over her mind he had understood it all, as plainly as if she had told it to him in so many words. She felt as if she would choke, and suddenly stood silent.

" What must I have thought of you ? " he repeated, smiling. " Nothing but good, you may be sure. Whatever becomes of Brian Holgate, he will not have wanted for a good woman's influence. Do not be troubled about that."

"But," she interrupted—she was standing up now, and stammered out—"you won't tell him all I said, sir. He might think I'd been too bold on his behalf, and——"

"I shall tell him nothing that you would not wish him to hear. What will you say to him? It is as well that I should know."

"Just that I came to see you, and that your secretary couldn't go with you, and I asked if you'd try him, and that you consented."

"Very well, that will do. And now, to consider the business part of the matter, I suppose you know that the *Batavia* sails to-morrow at two in the afternoon. I had already taken a berth for the gentleman whom I mentioned to you, so it will do

very well for him. I will see to the transaction—do you understand ? "

" Yes, sir, I understand."

" Very good. Then let him be at
Liverpool, and at the Cunard wharf, not
later than half-past twelve to-morrow.
And I think that is all. I need not keep
you any longer. Would you like to see
Mrs. Reichardt again before you go ? "

" No, not to-day ; I'll see her another
time. I couldn't talk to any one till I've
got this all settled," she said ; and Felix
almost laughed to himself at the relief he
felt at hearing this—he did not want Elisabeth to hear what he had done till Alice
Ormerod had left the house ; and, with a
guilty kind of feeling, he reconnoitred the
country before letting Alice out. The hall
was empty, the house was quiet ; he was
ashamed of himself for not having the
courage to ring the bell and have her

shown out in orthodox fashion ; but it was much easier, and, above all, much quicker, to walk across the hall with her, and himself to open the door for her. He answered her silent look of gratitude and tremulous emotion—half joy, half sorrow—with a smile, and a kindly pressure of the hand. She walked quickly away, and then he, feeling very much like a schoolboy who has been on a clandestine errand to the larder, returned to the sitting-rooms, and wandered from one to another of them, in search of his greatest friend.

He found her at last in her own sanctum, craved an audience, and was admitted. She was at her writing-table, but turned round as he came in.

"Well, do you want me to go down to her, or do you wish first to explain what her business was with you ? " she asked cheerfully.

"She has gone. Insulting though you may feel it to be to yourself, the truth is, she said she did not wish to see any one else—this time—after we had settled matters."

"What was her trouble then? Something that you could settle without my assistance, it seems. Oh, and Felix," she added briskly, "I have thought of a secretary for you—an excellent one. Yes, one of Mr. Reedley's young men. You are always so nasty about Mr. Reedley's young men, or I should have sent him word straight away to come here at once."

"It is a mercy you did not. It would have caused a complication, for I have just engaged a—well, I don't know whether secretary is just the right word—a companion, we'll say. Not one of Mr. Reedley's young men, but one recommended by Miss Alice Ormerod."

" What on earth do you mean ? "

" Our friend Brian Holgate is to go out with me."

" Brian Holgate ! What nonsense are you talking, Felix ? "

" It is not nonsense at all." He briefly related the story of his interview with Alice, and what she had asked, and what he had consented to do, and added, " It will be a bore, that's the worst of it—a frightful bore ; otherwise, it will answer • well enough, I dare say."

If he had hoped to avert the expression of her opinion by speaking in this off-hand way, he failed signally. She was silent for a few moments, looking at him. Then, slowly—

" Do you mean to tell me, sir, that this is serious—this tale I have heard, and not some wild and far-fetched romance ? "

" Perfectly serious. Why not ? "

" Because it is simply and utterly mad, and you are usually a sane person—*usually* —I don't say always."

" Mad ? What nonsense ! " said the much-tried man, who was leaning with his back against the mantelpiece ; and he moved his foot uneasily to and fro.

" It is mad, and it is nonsense. Don't really tell me you are committed to this thing, and can't get out of it."

" I have no wish to get out of it," he assured her, but not with very great heartiness. Then, with more decision, " But if I had, it is impossible. I have passed my word to her, and there is no going back from that."

She shrugged her shoulders, lifted her hands from her lap, and let them fall again with a mixture of annoyance and resignation in her expression.

" It is too bad—it is beyond everything," she said.

" I don't understand you. You used to profess the greatest interest in this very young man."

" Perhaps I did. I don't say that I am not interested in him even now. It's a very sad tale, I'm sure," said Elisabeth, with a sympathetic sigh. " But that is an entirely different thing—that is not the same as for you, Felix Arkwright, to set off on this journey, on which you will be criticised, and interviewed, and talked. about, and have everything belonging to you dragged into the greatest publicity, with a man who has just gambled away nearly all his estate, out of weak love for a bad girl, and who is now in the first despair and depression of the catastrophe. It is you who will have to look after him, instead of having in him a useful person to take all worry and trouble off your shoulders."

"I am not so sure it will be so bad as that," he said. "It will be a bore, I don't deny. But if I don't mind——"

"If you don't mind, I do," she told him, her colour rising, and her eyes filling with tears of vexation. "You are indifferent about appearances very often, I know, and so am I—about myself, but not where you come in, Felix. You can't make yourself into a mere private person travelling for pleasure, and you ought to have some regard for your *entourage*, for our sakes, if not for your own. I wanted all belonging to you to be *perfect*, and beyond all criticism, while you are over there. And now—you have let this creature be hooked on to you in this style. There's something so utterly incongruous about it. I could cry with vexation."

When Elisabeth got so far as to call a person suffering from misfortune a "creature," she must, indeed, have been deeply perturbed.

"Believe me, Lisa, I shall be equal to the emergency. I knew you would be vexed; and I am sorry, but I am not quite unversed in the ways of the world, after all. Your friend Alice put it very justly, when she said it might be the saving of him, body and soul. I gave her to understand that if I found him troublesome, or interfering in any way with my convenience, I should feel at liberty to send him away at once."

"It is done," was all that Elisabeth would say, "and it cannot be undone. But I hate it. I am certain no good will come of it, and if it were not your last day here I would quarrel with you."

"Don't do that," he said humbly, but smiling at the same time, in a way that increased her exasperation, so that she cried—

"Well, after this, never preach to me about acting on impulse, and saddling myself with all kinds of unprofitable burdens—never, sir. Nothing that I ever did could approach the recklessness of this."

"Then you admit that you have done reckless things ? "

"I admit nothing, except that you have called some of my actions reckless, while I know certainly that this of yours is sheer insanity. I have a good case against you now," she added triumphantly. "Ines was always a sore subject with you. By the use of your superior masculine overbearing strength, you bullied me out of alluding to that business in any but the most respectful way. But this—eleven years later—so much older, and no wiser—no more prudent, no more attached to your own interests—you shall not bully me out of this. I'll punish you with it many a time when you are so odious about my Mr. Reedley. So there! I dare say you will have saved the young man from destruction. I shall say no more about it, but I utterly disapprove of it."

With which she held out her hand. He came forward, stooped over it, carried it to his lips. "This kindly hand," said he, "has ever treated me more gently and generously than I deserved. And I don't think its owner means to strike me very hard, even now."

"Its owner is a weak-minded, silly woman, where her friends come in. And you have struck me hard enough this morning—and twice over. First about Ines, and now this. Well, well!"

CHAPTER X.

"BATAVIA," FOR NEW YORK.

ELISABETH'S party that evening was a
brilliant success.   It was not a very large
gathering—indeed, she said she hoped it
resembled the entertainments spoken of
by one of Miss Austen's heroines as
"small, but very elegant."   There was
some music, but not too much ; some
allusions, not to the coming parting, but
to the prospective triumphs of the singer
who was going away from them.   Felix
sang one or two songs of a rigorously
cheerful description, and Elisabeth per-
formed a perfect *tour de force* of brilliant
execution (execution and nothing else, as

she herself said) on her violin; a fantasia,
dazzling, and quite devoid of sentiment or
of anything but—execution.

There were some very pretty women
present, and there was a very fine supper
to be eaten, and very good champagne to
be drunk. And just before the last-
named event—the eating of the supper—
took place, a young girl who was present
implored Elisabeth to get Felix "to sing
' Auld lang syne,' or ' Home, sweet Home,'
or something like that, dear Mrs. Reichardt.
They say he can sing ballad music as
beautifully as he does everything else."

Elisabeth tapped her arm reprovingly
with her fan.

" What an idea, child ! As if such things
as this had any connection with ' Home,
sweet Home !' He is not going to
' Home, sweet Home,' but to America, to
New York; the thing I have just been

playing, exactly foreshadows in music what his career over there will be. You should never try to mix tears with laughter; it spoils the unity of things. And you must see that British ballad music and Frenchified New Yorkism don't go together."

The young lady blushed deeply, and was fain to withdraw and hide her diminished head, feeling as if she had done a very stupid thing. It was not Elisabeth's way to mortify the smallest or most insignificant of her fellow-creatures in this manner, but as a matter of fact, she was in a nervous agony lest any ill-advised person should actually prefer such a request to Felix, and lest he should comply with it. It would, she felt, have been quite too much for her. But, luckily, no such catastrophe occurred. The lively evening was kept up till a late hour, so that when her last guest was gone, she felt quite justified in pretending to be overcome with sleep and weariness; in apparently stifling a yawn, and with a kiss to her father-in-law, and a fleeting touch of her fingers on those of her friend, hastening away to her room.

They were all late the next morning, and there was not opportunity for much talk before it was time to go to the train which was to take them to Liverpool.

"Don't you think it will tire you very much, Lisa?" he asked her casually, when she said it was high time to go and put on her bonnet.

"No, I don't. I think it would be much more tiring to sit here thinking about it until *der Vater* returned to tell me all about it. And I don't care"—with sublime inconsistency—"if it should be ever so tiring; I am going to see the last of you, Felix, at Liverpool, and mind you don't forget to telegraph from New York."

He said no more. She went and put on her bonnet, according to her word; her carriage came round, and they drove down to the Irkford station, where they found several friends awaiting them who went with them to Liverpool, and there, of course, more were assembled. Elisabeth felt her composure returning; there was safety in numbers. It goes without saying that a friendship like this of Elisabeth and Felix had not been carried on without many a speculation on the part of those who witnessed it, as to whether it would not, should not, must not, end in a marriage; and they, being neither children nor simpletons, were perfectly aware of these speculations. Had such a thought existed, on either side, the alliance must quickly have come to an end; but no such

did exist, and their friendship remained—
a joy and a consolation to both. At this
moment the thought which chiefly agitated
Elisabeth's mind, was not one connected
with herself or her own privileges, but a
totally different one. She, Felix, and her
father-in-law were alone in the cab which
conveyed them from the Liverpool station
to the landing-stage. Here was her opportunity. She was just about to speak,
when Felix observed—

" I wonder if poor Holgate will be there
all right ? Rather a sell for me, if he
should not turn up after all."

A shade came over her face, and a smile
at the same time. " Oh, dear, I had
quite forgotten him ; and you must go
and bring him back to me just now, of
all times ! Of course he will be there.
That proverb about a bad shilling is the
truest one that was ever made."

He laughed.

"I must certainly keep him out of your way, or you will frighten him into going back."

"I wish I could. But a truce to your Holgates! Listen, Felix; I have something to say to you, and this is the only chance for me. I shall be writing to Ines in a day or two, and, of course, I shall mention having seen you off on this occasion, and, equally of course, she will have read all about your departure in the papers ever so long before. But in my letter may I not give her your love, and say that you told me to wish her good-bye?"

He was on the point of answering, "Oh yes, if you like;" but, happening to look at her before he spoke, he was struck with something of eagerness and excitement in her face and eyes, and his words were arrested. He paused a moment, then said—

"Now, look here, Lisa, my compact with that child was that absolutely *no* communications should pass between us —neither word, nor letter, nor message. She is prepared to carry out her share in the bargain like a Spartan. What would she think of me if I were the first to break them—the conditions I had myself laid down ? "

"She would think it adorable of you, I've no doubt."

"You are a very trying person, some-times ; and for quiet, persistent determina-tion to have your own way, I don't know your equal," he said, his colour rising. "But, as I should very much object to her thinking anything I did adorable, I must beg you not to break the agreement that we made with each other ; it will be altogether without my sanction if you say anything of the kind to her."

" I don't know how you can be so—so *granite* in your obduracy," she said vexedly, leaning back and looking crossly at him.

" Leave me alone," he answered her. " I am convinced that I am doing right, and that it will all turn out well in the end ; and, if you will leave it all to me, you won't be responsible if anything should go wrong."

" No," said she ; " but I am not happy about it. It haunts me sometimes."

To this he made no reply, and just at this moment their cab pulled up with a jerk. They had arrived at the wharf, and a porter threw open the door.

" *Batavia*," said Felix, briefly, glad to change the subject.

" *Batavia*—this way, sir. The last tender's waiting, and you haven't too much time."

And indeed they had not. They had scarcely hurried on to the tender, when the whistle sounded and they were off. Then Felix bethought himself suddenly of his promised travelling companion, and with a start and a muttered exclamation, he moved a little aside from his friends, reconnoitring the other groups present. Elisabeth guessed at once the reason of his moving away, and her jealous eyes followed him. He had not far to go. Then Elisabeth saw him accost a young man who had been standing alone, and who now made a step forward. They shook hands. Elisabeth looked, and despite her vexation, partly real, partly assumed, over this part of the business, she started and felt, first astonishment, then pity, as she began to admit to herself that she supposed this must be their pleasant host, Brian Holgate; but that if she had met him in the street she would assuredly have passed him without recognizing him. She recollected a kindly eyed, smiling lad, with a fresh colour and a cheerful aspect; she saw a still-looking man with a thin face, very white, and with eyes that seemed to have sunk far back into their sockets— mournful, haunting eyes. He looked so old, quite calm and self-possessed; but he reminded her of a man she had once seen who had just passed the turning-point in a fearful struggle between life and death, in what had been nearly a mortal illness. Brian Holgate's face had just that expression, she felt—as if the foe had been choked and flung aside, but as if another such victory would be far worse than a defeat. Perhaps, knowing the circumstances, she read something more than would have been apparent to an ignorant onlooker; but be that as it may, the feeling described seized her strongly. A very slight smile crossed his face as Felix came up to him. The artist also had felt a shock as he encountered those changed eyes of Brian's. It was not in his nature to do things by halves, and he held out his hand cordially, saying—

"We came so late, that I had not time to look for you before. I'm glad you have come, and we will have some talk a little later, on the steamer, shall we ?"

"Oh yes," said Brian, quietly. "Pray do not notice me till you have said good-bye to your friends. I preferred to come alone, and I will gladly wait till you are free."

Felix assented, and was turning away, when Elisabeth came up. Her vexation —what there was of it—had disappeared ; it never lasted long in the presence of grief or misfortune. Felix was surprised at the pleasure he felt when he saw her come forward, with the look of kindness on her face which he knew so well. She too went up to Brian and held out her hand.

"You remember me, Mr. Holgate, I hope?"

"Oh yes!" Brian's hat came off, and he made a profound bow; but, like all his words and his actions, it seemed mechanical.

"Go away, Felix," she said, smiling, to him; and, as he turned back to his friends, she continued, "Since you are going with him, Mr. Holgate, no matter under what circumstances, I want to tell you that I hope you will do what you can to help him. You will find him so easy to get on with—so kind and so considerate. Remember that there are some of us over here who would break our hearts, more or

less, if anything really bad were to happen
to him.   Will you?"

"Yes, Mrs. Reichardt; whatever lies in
my power I will do, so long as we are
together."

"And bring both him and yourself
safely back to us?"

"No doubt he will come safely back to
you.   As for me, I shall never return to
England."

"Oh yes, you will!" she said gently.
"Perhaps for you as well as for him there
are people whose hearts would break."
(He looked at her a little defiantly.)
"You will come back.   We shall see you
again."

Brian was silent.   In his mind's eye he
saw the scene of the morning—the cold,
dull, autumn dawn, the hurried prepara-
tions; the last look over the fields and
hills which he had loved so well; Sarah

Stott's woebegone mien ; his own words
to Alice—"Whatever you do on my behalf, Alice, will be right to me, and far
more than I deserve "—and her pale but
composed countenance, her unbroken self-
possession, her unfailing presence of mind
up to the very last, when she had laid her
hand upon his shoulder, kissed him gently,
and said, " Good-bye, and God bless you,
Brian, in all your undertakings." And
then the departure. He did not remember
much since that moment of Alice's kiss.
It seemed to him that from that instant all
his past was past—dead and buried, and
that never more would he wish or try to
revisit the scenes in which it had been
acted.

" I won't talk to you," said Elisabeth,
still more gently. " I only wanted to tell
you that I have never forgotten how kind
you were to us that day, and I shall never

forget you. I shall always expect Mr. Arkwright to tell me something about you, when he writes. And I shall not be long in going over to Thornton; I want to see Alice Ormerod again."

He smiled a little. "She'll be very glad," said he. "She thinks a deal of you, and has often said so."

Shaking his hand again, she wished him health and prosperity, and returned to her party. They had steamed into the shadow of the *Batavia's* great black hull. Half an hour later, the crowd of passengers on board the big liner were leaning over the taffrail, exchanging hand-kisses, waving of hats and handkerchiefs, and whispered last words, with tear-dimmed eyes, and in broken voices with the other crowd on the deck of the rapidly diminishing tender, as it relentlessly flew up the river to the town again. Then it was gone, and, so far as most of them knew, before any of those dear hands could again be clasped, or lips kissed, or voices heard, twice three thousand miles must be measured, and all the perils of the deep encountered.

Felix, as he turned away, and looked seawards, had a little uneasy feeling in his heart for a moment, no more.

" I almost wish I had said yes, to Lisa, when she asked for that message."

PART IV.

CHAPTER I.

THE contrast was a sharp one between those delightful days at Irkford and at Lanehead, and those at Madame Prénat's, which followed my return to her and to the town. But I congratulated myself many a time on my decision to come here, rather than remain there. If for some time after Felix's departure I found it desolate even here, where I had all my studies and occupations around me, and work with which to fill up most of the hours of the day, what would it have been at Lanehead, where I should have been supposed to be amusing myself and taking

a holiday, and where I should in reality
have been feeling, every hour, every day,
the absence of what, I had suddenly
discovered, was my most precious thing ?

After all, it was not so long since I had
left these grey squares and monotonous
streets. I had gone away for a certain
specified time, and I had returned before
that time was over. But I had, it seemed
to me, lived through a lifetime, since Felix
and I had driven away to Euston Square
that October afternoon. It was October
still. Only ten days later in the month.
But years had surely fled since then !
Madame, as I said before, did not en-
courage sentimentality, and I was grateful
to her that she did not. I had no wish to
mope, to dream, or to *afficher* my feelings
on the subject of what was, to me, the
great event of my life, this separation from
Felix, this time of probation which had

begun, and which stretched long and
painful before me. I went over the whole
interview many times in my own mind, but
could come to no definite conclusion as to
the reason of his sudden action. I could
trust him. I felt that more and more as
the days went on. I was sure he was not
anxious "to get rid of me," as I put it to
myself ; and he had told me emphatically
that I had not been guilty of any fault or
offence. Perhaps, some time, I should
know the reason of all this. I would
endeavour, in the mean time, so to act as
to please him, should he ever inquire into
the matter, and after a time I began to
hear and learn many things of which I
had been ignorant before, and to understand the mighty power of the two little
words, " they say."

For I soon found that I was no longer
a mere schoolgirl. The first thing that I

heard after my return was, that the two or three other girls who had at different times shared Madame's instructions and cares, were not coming back any more. It was some time since there had been any one but myself with her, and one day, after a call from one of those young ladies, who had apparently plunged into a busy social life at home, I asked Madame if we were going to be alone for the future.

"Yes," she told me; "I have decided it so. When Mr. Arkwright confided to me his wishes about you, and I resolved to accede to his request, I——"

"Won't you tell me what his wishes were?" I interrupted eagerly. She smiled.

"Oh, they were simple and comprehensive—men don't bother you with a lot of details. He hoped I would take charge of you, make you happy, or let you be happy in your own way, give you plenty

of employment, and take you into society
to a moderate extent. A woman would
have trusted me, perhaps, quite as much,
really, but she would have had all kinds of
instructions to give about not letting you
become a blue-stocking, or about your
dress, or—oh, fifty things. I saw what he
meant, of course. I consented to do it,
and at the same time I decided not to
receive any more of these young ladies.
As you well know, it is not essential to me
to have them with me—I mean from a
pecuniary point of view. I am not dependent upon it. It has always been a
work of love with me—this instruction,
this *education*—building up, as I trust it
most truly has been and always will be
with me. When I found I might rely
upon having you with me for two years,
you, in whom I was more interested than
in any of the others, and when I found

also that it was not merely to learn lessons
that you were to be placed with me, why,
then I told myself, ' I will give myself that
pleasure. I will have Ines Gray to myself.
I shall feel to her like a mother, and I
hope she will be able to confide in me
often, almost as a daughter, or perhaps
even more easily.' It is not always the
mother to whom we naturally turn with
our sorrows or our joys. And I trust,
my child," she added kindly, " that if you
ever feel in a difficulty, of any kind what-
soever, whether it may have been caused
by your own rashness and inexperience,
or by the wrong conduct of others, you
will never fear to speak to me of it. I
do not think you have ever found me
harsh or unsympathetic, and I do not
think you ever will. What I should resent in you would be not that you had
committed a fault, but that you had not

trusted me enough to speak to me of your
trouble."

" Dear Madame Prénat," I exclaimed,
" I hope I shall never disappoint your
kindness to me." And, indeed, I was
profoundly touched, and felt that no
devotion on my part could be too great
in repayment of this kindness.

" With Mr. Arkwright," she pursued,
" one feels on such sure ground. He
says, ' I trust you—I confide in you,' and
you are not annoyed by afterwards finding
that he meant, ' except in this matter, that
matter, or the other matter.' Yes "—she
nodded her head—" I think we shall get
on and be happy together."

At night I mused over the subject. I
had not yet grasped the full bearings of
the situation. Felix, it appeared, had
absolute confidence in Madame Prénat ; I
knew Elisabeth had. He seemed to have

expressed his views to her very fully. It came into my mind for the first time to wonder when this negotiation had taken place—how long had it been in his mind to take this course? Had it been decided before I received that letter from him about going to Irkford? I would have given a good deal to know, but he had said nothing about it. Madame never mentioned it, and it seemed to me disloyal to pry into the matter. It had been decided thus :—for two years I was to live with Madame Prénat, and do my best to attain to her standard of young woman-hood, which was by no means a low or easy one. At the end of two years I was to see Felix again. After that—sometimes I wondered a little, but stifled my wonder-ings. It would be all right, I did not doubt.

I was over seventeen; consequently the

first schoolroom drudgery was past. What
remained before me, the work that Madame
laid out for me, and upon which I eagerly
fastened, was a kind of modified college
course, carried on at her house, under her
supervision; partly under her own instructions, for she was profoundly versed
in some branches of education—in history,
for example, and in some departments of
literature; partly under the tuition of
different professors. She had a gift which
amounted to genius for rapidly discerning
exactly what capacities, moral, social, and
intellectual, a person possessed; for putting
her finger with unerring certainty on just
those which it would be worth while to
cultivate, the cultivation of which would be
likely to improve, strengthen, and purify
the character; and those which, on the
other hand, might be safely left alone, as
not likely to repay tillage, so to speak, by

the production of any flowers of sweetness and light, larger sympathy, or truer ways of thinking. She was a great advocate for the training of the faculties all round, so as to enable their owner to make good use of them in any given circumstances, as opposed to the admired system of cram on some one or two points, in order to pass competitive examinations, which system finds such favour, glory, and applause in these latter days. And with this gift of discernment she possessed also strong and passionate convictions on such subjects as worthy objects in life, and a constant striving after perfection. To her views on these subjects people sometimes objected that it would not pay to follow them, however admirable they might be. Success in her much-hated competitive examinations as often as not meant success in the battle of life which had to follow

after them.   Failure in the same, however
well-equipped the individual might be in
the line of education which she advocated,
meant failure to find any place in the
foremost ranks of society, the professions,
or the services—for men ; and girls were
rapidly following in the same direction.
To which her answer always was, in tones
of resignation, that she knew it ; she did
not pretend to stem the torrent single-
handed—not she : it was an impetuous, if
a shallow one.   But, fortunately for her,
there still existed thoughtful and intelligent
persons of her way of looking at these
things—and often they were also persons
of means and leisure.   Many such persons
had committed their daughters to her
charge at different times, and she trusted
that each one of those girls went forth into
the world with some truer notions as to
real education than that it was a mad

struggle to know more on a given day, of a given subject, than was known by the other feverish competitors for the same thing. The leaven might work slowly, but it would work, she knew, and she could die happy in the conviction that she had, whenever the least opportunity offered, introduced it and worked it well into the characters she had been privileged in any degree to form.

At such times, when giving us these her views, Madame's countenance took an almost rapt expression, the expression of an enthusiast. Her large, soft, near-sighted eyes would light and glow, her abundant white hair—for it was white, though she was not yet fifty—looked like a silvery nimbus about her strong, noble face, and I, listening, felt all the influence of a powerful, mature enthusiasm upon my own young and as yet untried ardour and passionate desire to live the good life, the true and the beautiful life, at what cost soever, no matter how often I might hear outsiders declare that "they say" Madame Prénat's views are high-flown nonsense.

As I have before related, I had not been with her many weeks after my first going to her, before she told me that my dutiful and diligent practice on the piano was exactly so much force wasted and time lost. How she also brought to bear upon me Felix's verdict to the same effect I have told. I never touched a piano again, and at the same time I never ceased to regret my utter incapacity as a musical performer.

Besides, she very soon caused me to discard all my arithmetical and mathematical studies, save the one useful accomplishment of being able correctly to add,

subtract, multiply, and divide. "When a
person has plenty of talent for other
things," she said, "and none whatever for
arithmetic, we must let him off the arithmetic, and let him know that we expect so
much the more from him in other branches
of knowledge." All artistic studies, in the
conventional sense of the word, she also
discouraged. I did not sketch in water-
colours, nor dab oils into the semblance of
feather beds and cabbages, and call them
waterfalls and trees ; I did not perpetrate
fantastic tricks with paints and brushes on
pots and plaques, and afterwards hang
them round the walls and look at them,
all unconscious of their hideousness—
which is the common doom of those who
do paint pots and plaques. I did not
hammer brass with diligence, nor hew
good wood into shapes of fruit and foliage
such as were never seen before or since

the Flood. I worked not in leather, nor in wax. Floss silks, coloured cottons, and Berlin wools were strange to my fingers, though I was not unacquainted with the useful needle and thread, and could sew a " white seam " with neatness and rapidity.

On the other hand, under her stringent supervision, I did gain a clear idea or two about the different periods of art ; the several schools, the main features of them, and the characteristics of the cele-brated masters who had flourished and figured in the world's history—from the builders of the Pyramids downwards. I did, I believe, get a quick and lively sense as to what was true and what was false art. I learnt something about history and literature ; some main facts concerning them, which I was not likely to forget.

And as for music,—though I had given over attempting to play the piano,—we

were by no means without relaxation in
this line. Very thoroughly did I enjoy
the concerts and the few operas to which
we went—never, though, to any in which
Felix was singing. I knew most of the
great tone-poems, and loved them—but
only the great ones. Indeed, in art, as in
everything else, I learnt, under Madame
Prénat's auspices, to feel an absolute
indifference for all that was not of the
very best. I scarcely felt contempt for
the second-rate—it hardly came home to
me at all. I was highly satisfied with
this state of things: it seemed natural and
right to care only for the best—not to
have any feeling at all for what fell below
that. It never occurred to me, and I am
sure it did not to her, that she was making
me into something so fastidious, by this
course of hot-house training (she would not
have called it hot-house training, though;

she would have said that this was the
education which helped nature into the
right road, and that the other it was which
was forced and exotic) that if, or when,
at any future time, I should have to
encounter things and persons not of the
very first order, come in contact with
them, and have dealings with them, the
awakening and the friction might chance
to be not merely pain but torture. In
the meantime, having swept away all
studies and accomplishments which in her
opinion were not suitable, she pushed on,
all the more eagerly, those which were;
and I, nothing loth, needed no spurring
on.

As I have already said, I found my
greatest pleasure in the study of the
oriental languages. These tongues had a
fascination for me, with their strange
characteristics and the wonderful glimpses

they gave into thoughts and ways of life which were not as ours. My chief instructor in these matters was a certain learned Professor Willoughby, a man of great fame as an orientalist, who was said to know more Sanskrit than any other man in the world. Had he and his wife not been personal friends of Madame Prénat's, I might have wished and sighed in vain for his guidance. As it was, they had dined with us one evening, when the Professor had been in a singularly good humour. Madame had casually mentioned some of my struggles in my study of Greek, and had roused the learned man's curiosity so far as to induce him to ask me some questions. I was nervous, but pleased. Before the Willoughbys departed that evening, he had told me to come to him at an early hour in the morning, a few days thence, when he

would see what I could do, and—implied,
though not spoken out—whether I was
worthy of having a little of his precious
time and learning bestowed upon me. I
went at the appointed time, and returned
radiant.

" Madame," I cried, " he will give me
an hour once a week; every Tuesday,
from nine to ten."

Madame looked at me. Her grave
face broke into a smile—the smile could
not be made to express all her feelings.
She took my hand, stooped forward, and
gave me a kiss.

" You have a future before you, Ines,"
she said, looking at me with an expression
full of satisfaction; " a real future, apart
from the crowd. Only keep your health
and work hard, but not recklessly, and it
lies before you to make a name, and a
name in what is for women a new field."

"I feel afraid when you say that," said I uneasily. "You think too much of what I can do, madame."

"You must not be afraid; there is no need to be afraid. You must think only of what you are doing—the work and not the goal."

Sometimes I asked her how much work one could accomplish, how much progress one could make, in two years.

"I wish you would not think of two years," she always said to me on such occasions. "Think rather of twenty; think of the years Professor Willoughby has devoted to these studies; how he has grown old and grey in them, and has, in such matters, an authority which no one would think of disputing; and yet, when you ask him what has been done in this task of exploring the oriental languages, and of establishing the science of language itself on a right basis, he smiles with pity and says, 'Ask, rather, what there is to do, and I should almost have to tell you —everything.'"

"But, Madame Prénat," I besought her, "I don't want to become old and grey yet in anything. I think it is a little too soon ; and I don't think of twenty years— two are quite enough for me."

I usually said this a little maliciously, in order to smile at the look of pain and reproach which always overspread her countenance when she heard these (to her) unworthy sentiments. But our little difference usually ended in my saying, as I took her hand,

"You will not say that I do not work now, madame, at any rate ?"

"No ; you are a good child ; you are diligent, you are thorough. You love your work as few girls have done whom

I have known. One must have one's dream, in youth above all. Yes, I had mine once—such a grand dream! *Mon Dieu!* Had it been fulfilled, what a weary old age I should have had! But, my child, the best of all were not to think of either two years or twenty years, but of to-day and to-morrow, and of how to make the most of them—how best to live them in every way."

"And that is what I really do, Madame Prénat," I assured her. "I should not be happy if I did otherwise."

What I said was true. And the day's work and occupations did really grow gradually more absorbing and interesting, till, as week after week went on, and Felix's name was never even mentioned, the strangeness of the silence began to wear off, and I to grow accustomed to it. But every day I never forgot, when I

had done reading aloud to madame the
summary of the day's news, and perhaps
one or two of the leading articles, to skim
over, for myself alone, other portions of
the journals—advertisements of concerts
and operas, criticisms, short notices of new
compositions; and seldom did I fail to
find, somewhere or other amongst them,
the name I was looking for. Yes, it
would seem that his life was in its way
as even and unvaried as our own; filled
day after day with the same things.
Triumphs even must grow monotonous in
time, I reflected. Be that as it might, I
learnt from these newspaper paragraphs
that he was still here, still well; moving
about from place to place, and leading
his life. That satisfied me. And at times
a letter from Elisabeth would give me
some little detail, all the pleasanter to
learn because she knew, and I knew, that

she was breaking the spirit, if not the letter, of our compact, in communicating it.

Such was one phase of my life at Madame Prénat's.

CHAPTER II.

" INES, don't forget that we are engaged this evening — the Farquharsons, you know."

" So we are. Need I really go, Madame Prénat ? "

" Yes. Why should you stay at home ? "

" It seems to me that we are always going out."

" By no means. Twice or thrice a week."

" One could do so much more if one stayed at home."

" Perhaps, for the time, one could ; and fall out of touch with all that is going on,

and live with your nose in your books, and
look bewildered when a man or a woman
in society speaks to you. What end do
you purpose to gain by making a hermit of
yourself ? "

" No, you are right, I suppose. And
the places I go to with you are always
interesting."

" Of course. The *vie de pensionnât de
demoiselles* is all very well for school-girls,
but not for you. Pray remember that you
are a young woman now, in the world, like
other young women ; if your occupations
and aims in life are somewhat different
from theirs, that is no reason why you
need show yourself eccentric and different
from others. That is such nonsense, and
usually such conceit; so make yourself
ready."

" Will my white cashmere do ? "

" Just as you like. You know what

Mrs. Farquharson's parties are; use your own judgment. You have plenty of frocks."

Slowly I went upstairs. Having put my books away, I got out my white cashmere gown and began the process of dressing, and while thus engaged I reflected upon her words—" a young woman in the world, like other young women." What were other young women like? I knew not. I had no friends amongst girls of my own age. Truth to tell, Elisabeth had spoiled me for taking much pleasure in girl-friendships; my whole life and surroundings had tended to keep me out of such friendships. They were very nice, very pretty, these young damsels that I met up and down, with their smooth faces, and eyes, demure or bright—gaze forthright or down-dropped as the case might be— but always, as it seemed to me, on the watch. What were they watching for, these maidens in the pretty fresh ball-dresses, the immaculate gloves and shoes? What was the meaning of that everlasting question in their eyes, the look of expectancy on their young faces? I never felt expectant or questioning — never! Perhaps that was what left me free to observe others and mark this peculiarity.

"—your aims and occupations in life are somewhat different from theirs." What, then, were their aims and occupations in life? So interested did I grow in the working out of this question, that I gradually became quite still, sitting on an ottoman at the foot of my bed, and, with my white shoelace dropping from my fingers, I gave my whole mind to the solution of the problem. At last a light flashed into my mind. Was it, could it be, that they, these girls in society—what-

ever that might mean—found, or hoped
or tried to find, husbands there? Was
that the meaning of it all? Did that
explain their watchful eyes? It could not
be true of all, but I was sure that it was
of many. That was their business, and,
if so, our aims and occupations were indeed
very different — yea, verily! I smiled
slightly to myself. No wonder that I did
not feel drawn to them; no wonder that
Professor Willoughby and Madame Prénat
and Elisabeth were to my mind far more
delightful company than the young ladies,
or than the young gentlemen, either, for
that matter. I would ask Madame Prénat
about it. I always asked her questions
about social matters which might puzzle
me. Perhaps she would give some other
solution to the problem than that which
had occurred to me; and yet I doubted
whether she could, except in regard to some

few unusual cases. I was sure I had hit upon the right answer to a great part of the riddle. No, that would never interest me; and yet, could things go on thus for ever? Even if I had, as I felt with profound conviction, no interest in the marriage market, still a time would come when I should have to face some other kind of life than this. I should not live for ever with Madame Prénat, I should not for ever continue to be the adopted child of Felix Arkwright, taking the benefits he poured upon me, as a child might, but as might only a child. I had no need to think closely about that till those two fateful years should have expired. But then I should have not only to think but to act. Perhaps my turn would come too—I might find some one asking me to marry him, all unexpectedly. Such things had happened to girls before. Again I shook

my head ; that would make no difference.
I was not going to be married.

Yet I had no claim upon any one except
my own relations. I shivered a little
when I thought of them, and of the scene
at the Festival at Kirkfence. The fear
which had then entered my heart, and had
chilled and terrified me, had been lest they
should ever think it worth their while to
seek me out, and offer now to do what
they had at first refused to do by me—
what might bluntly be called their duty.
I hoped that day might never come.

These girls whom I met either got their
husbands, I supposed, and went off into
homes of their own, and were no more
heard of; or, if not that, then, as they
became older, they left the market-place and
retired into private life with their parents
or their relations. At any rate they were,
mostly, provided for. I was not. The

"future" of which Madame Prénat had spoken, now began to have some meaning for me. Now I understood why I was not to think in particular of two years, but rather of twenty—of the future in general. It had become suddenly clear. I had had a happy life, happier, I felt sure, than the lives of most girls (but I admit that I reasoned on this matter from very imperfect data). I did not feel afraid of the future, but I saw it stretching before me, full of serious purpose, full of gravity, full of responsibility, full of work.

"Are you ready, Ines? I have been waiting more than ten minutes. What on earth has the child been pottering with?"

"I beg your pardon!" I exclaimed, in deep confusion. "I will be ready in ten minutes." And in that space of time we were being quickly driven to our destination.

I remember that evening well, and, indeed, I have good cause to remember it. It was the beginning of a new phase in my existence, of a kind to which I had scarcely ever given even a passing thought. The party was at the house of a Mrs. Farquharson, whose husband was a journalist of repute, chief editor of a well-known London daily newspaper. Mrs. Farquharson's parties were usually worth going to, more or less, and the people one saw there were worth meeting; for this reason, if for no other, that her company really was good of its kind—genuine and not imitation. If one met a learned professor at her house, he *was* a learned professor and not some one who had merely met a great many learned professors, and listened to them talking, and thought them very interesting, but did not know very much about their subjects himself. If you were

introduced there to a politician who had
" something to say about Ireland," for in-
stance, you might rely upon it that he did
know something about Ireland from one
point of view, at any rate, if not from
more. The facts he might tell you would
be facts ; of course there might be many
more facts of another kind of which he
knew, or told you, nothing, but you might
rely upon what you heard from him, as far
as it went. And so it was with them all,
artists, specialists in some department of
science, literature, or research : it was
seldom you met any one really insignificant
in that house. And another pleasing
feature about these entertainments was
that they were rarely, if ever, overcrowded.

We found a rather larger company than
usual there on our arrival. Soon after we
went in, our hostess led a gentleman up
to me and introduced him as Dr. Her-

mann Barthel.   I knew his name; he was
a young German who had already made
great fame as an orientalist, and as an
explorer of some of the " buried cities of
the East."   We fell into conversation at
once.   Professor Willoughby was a common friend, and we talked first of him,
and then went on to other topics.

" I have some photographs—some remarkable photographs of some of the
tombs at ——," he said at last.   " With
your leave I go to fetch them from that
other room, and return to you with them.
You would like to see them ? "

" Oh, very much, thank you," I assured
him, and, springing up with alacrity, he
went towards the small, inner drawing-
room.   Madame Prénat was deep in conversation with some man whom I did not
know, at the other end of the room.   I
leaned back in the vis-à-vis in which I was

sitting, and slowly fanned myself, while
I awaited the return of Dr. Barthel with
the photographs.

Voices behind me presently drew my
attention. A lady and a gentleman spoke
together.

" You were there too ? " he asked, in a
tone of interest.

" Yes, of course. I never miss going to
hear him, when I can possibly manage it
—Felix, I mean. It was very fine, I
thought, but then, what a splendid cast
altogether ! "

I became all ears, unscrupulous ears, at
this.

" Yes ; but I think it is a pity that he
should begin with that kind of thing, unless
he means to go on with it exclusively.
And his voice really is too magnificent
to be ruined by a course of Wagner
opera," said the gentleman, who spoke

the words "Wagner opera" in no very loving tones.

"Oh, that is not fair. Music like that deserves that those who interpret it should be the best of their kind, and should bring the best they have to the interpretation."

"I hear you are a convinced devotee of the Master," said he, laughing. "One might dispute about it for ever. I don't share your views on the matter, and I don't want Felix to spoil his voice, even to give us a finer Count Telramund than any one else could."

"Ah, it was that, most certainly. It may be unwise in him, but I'm glad I've lived to hear it."

"And the Ortruda?"

"Equally fine. Reuter certainly *can* sing Ortruda like no one else."

"She was in a good humour," he said provokingly, "because she was singing with

Felix. You know, she likes singing with Felix."

Yes, she does, I assented within myself. Had my own eyes not seen it ?

They laughed.

" Does he like singing with her ? " asked the lady.

" I should suppose so, unless he is impervious to the charm of a beautiful woman with a beautiful voice, who uses it as only a great artist can. And one would hardly predicate that of him."

" No, I suppose not. She is a beautiful woman, without doubt."

" It is true that he is not over fond of his profession—the dramatic part of it, at any rate. He once told me so himself."

" Really ! With all his popularity ? "

"Yes, with all his popularity, and all his genius, too."

"Don't you think that may be a bit of affectation?"

"Oh no, I'm sure it isn't. He is not affected. There have been other instances of the kind, you know. There was Macready, and there was Fanny Kemble, to take only two of them. He hates the stage part of the business. But I don't think he ever makes any fuss about it."

"Still," persisted his companion, "he may dislike his profession ever so much, and yet enjoy singing with Madame Reuter."

"Oh yes!" he laughed a little. "I know nothing at all about that. But I know she likes singing with him."

"Yes. Well, he certainly is wonderful. He's the only one amongst the singing men and singing women, who has ever drawn tears from my eyes since "—she paused—" since I became a hardened old woman of the world—you know what I mean." Her voice took an accent of weariness.

The conversation altogether hinted at a background known to both of them— a blank to me. But I thought, " O charming woman of the world ! Dear fashionable stranger ! Are there many like you ? "

There was a little pause between them. Then he said again—

" Willoughby was telling me of a pupil of his who was to be here to-night—a young and lovely and learned person, by whom he sets great store. He says she has an absolute genius for oriental languages, and that he takes more interest in her and expects more from her than from any of the men who attend his lectures at the University ; and he believes that if she has her health and doesn't go and get married—his words, I assure you, with his wife standing by—she will leave them all behind, too."

Shortly before the end of this speech it began to dawn upon my mind that I was the pupil in question. My face grew hot. One very pleasant reflection came to me—that it was really true, or the Professor would never have spoken so of me to this stranger. Some day I should be able to do something. In the mean time I fidgeted and felt uneasy, and began to wish that Dr. Barthel would return with those photographs; which, indeed, he seemed to have been a long time in finding. Perhaps he had fallen in with some-one on the way, and was expounding the mysteries of his pictures to that some-one, oblivious of my very existence.

The lady stifled a yawn.

"Ah," said she, with great indifference, "that isn't much in my line. Another of your 'sweet girl-graduates.' One hears of so many now, but somehow they never seem to come to anything. What does become of them? Are they the women who write the books, or paint the pictures, or turn out great actresses and singers? I've often wondered."

Evidently girl-graduates did not interest her (nor me either, for that matter) so much as the question whether or not Felix liked singing with Madame Reuter.

"Oh, well, you put such sweeping questions. There are hundreds of girl-graduates, and Willoughby has hundreds of pupils, of one sort or another. But he doesn't take that profound interest in them all, and she isn't at college, either. She's not going in for cram. She is living with Madame Prénat; and, by the way, it's

quite a romantic history "—he started up
—"now I will tell you a tale that ought to
endear me to you for ever.   Listen——"

It was unbearable.   I dared not sit and
listen to any more of it.   I rose, intending
to cross the room to Madame Prénat, and
had made two or three steps away from
the two friends, when it seemed that some
one was standing exactly in front of me,
and a voice said to me—

"Good evening, cousin Ines.   Will
you look at me, and kindly try to recall.
me to your recollection?   We have met
before."

Startled, I looked up at the speaker,
who was taller than I, and recognized the
grave, pale face, and dark grey eyes of the
young man called Maurice, who had insisted upon an introduction to me at the
musical festival, and whom I had been
glad to forget, along with his companions,

as much as possible. He looked at me
and held out his hand.

"Will you not shake hands with me ?
I have seen Madame Prénat, and she sent
me here to find you."

END OF VOL. II.